PO 40
X

# BORDERLAND HOMECOMING

# BORDERLAND
# HOMECOMING

•

## Ellen Gray Massey

*AVALON BOOKS*
NEW YORK

PRINTED IN THE UNITED STATES OF AMERICA
ON ACID-FREE PAPER
BY HADDON CRAFTSMEN, BLOOMSBURG, PENNSYLVANIA

To my brothers Harold and Ralph Gray
for their continual support and encouragement

## Chapter One

Riding point, Schell Campbell's probing gaze over the prairie spotted the lone blue hill on the horizon. He straightened and squinted to see better as he quickened his horse's pace. His apprehension, which had been building for the last two days of his cattle drive south from Independence, Missouri, was obvious to Walking Owl who had swung to the rear of the herd to urge on the stragglers.

Unconsciously Schell had been increasing his speed in his hurry to reach home. The tautness of the pack mules' lead rope, the dog's barking at the straggling cattle, and Walking Owl's shrill call to them made him realize how fast he was going. Schell checked Solomon's speed, turned in his saddle toward Walking Owl, and whistled.

When the Osage man rode up beside his companion, Schell pointed southwest toward the hill. "There it is, Walker. There's Campbell's Hump! I'm home!" He let out a "Yahoo," and waved his Union Army hat into the air, grinning boyishly. The worry lines around his eyes that had been carved by four years of the Civil War disappeared, revealing a vigorous young man of twenty-six.

1

"Yeah," the older man said, equally pleased. "I see it."

"Is it like your tribe's ancestral mounds?"

"It's similar. Like I remember from my last trip back to this country with my father thirty-five years ago. That was my first expedition as an adult. I was fifteen."

They were cutting across the country on the firm sod of bluestem grass, already tall enough to wave in the late-April breeze. "How's it different?"

"This land is flatter. But your treeless, mound-like hill over there sticking up over the landscape, that and the grass, they are the same as my old homeland over there at the edge of the woodland hills." He waved his arm toward the east.

As far as the men could see the world was carpeted with gray-green grass, sprinkled with joyful yellow buttercups and bluets. Arched over all was the deep, sparkling blue of a spring sky. Campbell's Hump was the only elevation on the horizon.

The two men rode side by side, each anticipating the end of their week-long trek. Stroking his dark beard, twisting and squirming impatiently in his saddle, Schell alternately whistled, "Soldier's Joy," and chatted. In contrast, Walking Owl glided quietly beside him as if molded to his bay horse. The Osage's hair-free face was serious, his dark eyes missing nothing in the open land—the labored breath of the two pack mules, the plodding herd behind them, the stirring in the prairie sod beneath them, the calls of the meadowlarks, and the piles of soft pellets that told the presence of deer.

Both men were anxious to get Schell's cattle safely to his father's ranch, where the Osage had agreed to stay a few weeks to help Schell get settled and prepare for the arrival of his eastern fiancée, Cynthia. Walking Owl was also considering settling here. But before he could think seriously about that, as the men agreed when they'd paired up two weeks before, Schell would accompany him to Blue Mounds. There Walking Owl would visit the burial place of his maternal grandfather, the great Osage chief, Pawhuska, or White Hair. Schell surmised that there was something else his partner wanted to do there—perhaps find something that dated back to before his father's death?

The men were absorbed in their thoughts, Schell's eyes on the distant hump and Walking Owl's studying the characteristics of the dry sod they were crossing. The Osage was the first to notice the unusual silence of the prairie birds, the growing restlessness of the cattle, and then to smell a difference in the air. Alarmed, he noticed some smoke in the west.

"Prairie fire!" he shouted to Schell. "Headed across our path." He scanned the horizon in every direction to find some shelter, for the southwesterly wind would drive the rapidly approaching fire right toward them.

Schell quickly assessed the situation. He had experienced fires in this country. Fire sparked by lightning or by man, would set off tall, dry grasses and burn unchecked across miles of open land, taking everything in its path. A glance at the now-visible blaze fast approaching told Schell that turning back was no solution. They could not outrun it.

He made himself remember the details of the landscape. "There's a little creek over southeast. Maybe we can beat the fire there," Schell said, pointing to a dark line of trees on the horizon.

Walking Owl reined his bay back to the herd before

Schell had finished talking. With orders to Harris, the dog, and shrill calls to the cattle, he forced them to a lope. Harris expertly nipped at the laggards' heels, avoiding their kicking hooves. Schell added his "Yah! Yah!" to the crescendo of barking, mooing, thundering hooves, and the Osage's high "Eye-yie-yie-yie-eye." The once peaceful prairie became a maelstrom of noise, dust, and smoke.

Schell's Solomon and Walking Owl's bay were galloping at full speed, circling on the east side and behind the running cattle and pack mules to keep them moving in a southerly direction. Hoping to beat the fire to the creek, they pushed the herd toward the fire, angling slightly to the east. The instincts of the cattle, and especially the two pack mules, warned the animals to run in the opposite direction, away from the blaze and smoke. Even Harris's orders had to be repeated time and again, for like the herd, he couldn't understand why they were racing so madly toward the danger.

Tongues of orange-red fire were lapping across the prairie, fed by last year's dead stalks. Familiar with these types of fires, the men knew that the fire's progress would be checked somewhat because the dry, dead stalks that fed the fire were surrounded by the new green growth. Though it was unseasonably dry, remnants of winter moisture clung to the ground, further slowing the fire. Had it been August, they would already have been consumed by walls of fire. If they could just keep the animals moving, they might reach the creek.

One cow and calf turned back. Another tried to follow. Walking Owl and Harris cut back the second cow, but could not catch the first.

"Let 'er go, Walker," Schell yelled, waving his arm toward the wooded line of the creek less than half a mile away.

Solomon jumped over a downed calf, almost pitching Schell from the saddle. Over the bawl of the stampeding herd, the men could now hear the roar of the fire. The smoke was making them choke even through the protective, red bandanna kerchiefs tied over their faces. The acrid smoke was burning their eyes. Some of the cattle were coughing.

Another cow and calf escaped from Harris, galloping wildly back the way they had come onto the open prairie ahead of the line of fire.

"Almost there!" Schell shouted, more to encourage the herd rather than to give information. Calling in Harris, they slowed their speed, so that the animals would not injure themselves by galloping out of control into the marshy land by the creek bank. Finally understanding that safety lay in this direction, the lead steer willingly entered the narrow line of trees. Walking Owl galloped to get ahead of him and then slowed down to spread the herd out in the narrow, wooded bank beside the creek bed until he found a safe place for them to cross.

The steep, muddy banks could cause injuries and pileups if the frightened cattle reached the area all at once at full speed. The Osage was slowly trotting his bay when he found a rocky ford. The lead steer stepped nimbly across the creek and climbed the sloping bank on the other side. The rest of the herd, urged by Harris and Schell, followed. Behind them, the fire skirted the wooded area of the creek and continued northeastward into the open grasses, blackening the route they had just traveled.

Exhausted, the cattle huddled together on the safe side

of the creek, their sides heaving, their heads low, and their eyes still wild. Harris, panting, flopped down on his side for a few minutes to catch his breath. Schell patted his wiry head. "Good boy," he said. Harris wagged his skinny tail. He then returned to the creek to lap up huge mouthfuls of the muddied water.

The men walked among the cattle to access damages.

"They're okay," Walking Owl said. "After a short rest and a good drink, they'll make it to your place before night."

Schell nodded his agreement. Only six head lost—not bad when he might have lost the whole herd.

"We were lucky," Walking Owl said.

Considering all the risks he'd taken since leaving Independence, not even counting the four years of war, Schell had to agree. A prairie fire was not the worst thing that could have happened.

"How do you suppose it started?" Schell asked.

Walking Owl thought for a moment, studying the sky and the southwestern horizon where the fire originated. "Wasn't lightning. I'd say this time of year with all the new growth, someone must have started it. Once started and encouraged, the dead grass would burn hot enough to take the new, but everything is too green now for an accidental fire like that one." He looked back through the trees across the creek at the cloud of smoke which was disappearing over the prairie swell toward Nevada City. Then he looked south at Campbell's Mound now clearly visible in the distance.

"Someone doesn't want us coming, would be my guess," Walking Owl said.

With the cattle quiet, the men found places to sit, their

backs to the smoking, charred land. Their interest now lay across the green prairie on the unburned side of the creek.

"Somebody doesn't want us coming!" The words seared through Schell, voicing his submerged fear. But his home mound was safe. The fire had started north of the little creek which ran basically east about seven miles north of Campbell's Hump. Impatient with this delay to let the animals rest before traveling on, Schell tried to pass the time with happy thoughts of the reunion with his parents and siblings, but he could only remember the troubled, almost ominous events of his trip home.

What would he find on that hazy, blue mound still too far away to see details? Had it shared the same fate of most of the places he'd seen? Just this morning, he had glimpsed Nevada City across the prairie. From the growing town he once knew, all he could spot still standing after the raids during the war was one pre-war house and the stone walls of the jail. There were a few new huts thrown up and some make shift buildings. But so anxious was Schell to get home, that he skirted the village without speaking to anyone.

Since leaving Independence, he and Walking Owl had found nothing but war desolation—skeletons of cattle and hogs, and chimneys standing alone beside ashy piles that once were homes, barns, and store buildings. This destruction was not from prairie fires, but deliberate burnings by both armies and outlaws. Most of the people they encountered were returning, like Schell, or were newcomers seeking land and opportunity now that the war was over. What few native Missourians they met looked with hostility at Schell's Yankee Army hat and coat and at Walking Owl's Union boots and Spencer rifle. Though Missouri had stayed in the Union, many people in the counties bordering Kansas were Confederate sympathizers.

Walking Owl warned Schell that in addition to this passive antagonism, open conflict continued between outlaws and renegades. "But, Walker, it's all over," Schell had said. "The war's been over for a year. As I came all the way from New York across Ohio, Indiana, and Illinois, I saw everywhere that life was returning to normal."

Walking Owl shook his head sadly. "Not here in Missouri it's not." Schell decided his older friend was unduly pessimistic, but agreed to avoid settlements and main roads, relying on their memories of the land to avoid any confrontation. But in case anyone challenged them, they had Colt, and Smith and Wesson pistols in their belt holsters and the multi-shot Spencer and Henry rifles strapped across their backs.

Meeting each other in Independence and joining forces to take Schell's herd to his ranch was the opportunity Walking Owl needed to return to the continental borderland where woods met the prairie. The past week had confirmed the men's initial liking for each other—the army lieutenant and the experienced Osage scout. They made a good team—younger Schell's impetuosity and Walking Owl's studied caution.

The outcome of the trip for Walking Owl hinged on his memory and the innate deductive ability of the Osage that his father nurtured in him years before. As he traveled south, his mood became more optimistic. If his time spent in the mission school and his subsequent years in the White world hadn't completely erased his ability, he might at long last find what he was now free to search for.

Schell, too, was basically optimistic. But overshadowing

the reunion and the happy plans for himself and his fiancée, was an uneasiness about his home. Though he visualized Cynthia's delight with the land when she arrived his
anxiety about his family increased as he traveled deeper
into the prairie regions of the southern Missouri counties
on the Kansas border.

Just before spotting the fire, with the sun burning away
the blue haze of Campbell's Hump, Schell had squinted
his eyes to see his father's house on top. Still too far away
to make out details, though he did notice that there were
a few trees—probably the elms and cottonwoods his
mother had planted for shade on the grassy mound. Schell
smiled remembering how his parents loved the view from
their new house.

As usual, Walking Owl said very little. The cattle, accustomed to traveling, followed meekly behind them once
they, were underway. Schell kept his eyes on The Hump,
as his family called the mound, knowing that Harris, the
scraggly mutt who had joined them when they passed the
village of Harrisonville would see to any strays.

Schell had paid little attention to Walking Owl's movements or to his friend's orders to Harris because of the
sinking feeling in his stomach, after seeing the mound in
the distance. Schell should be able to see the house by
now. His brothers should have spotted him, since from the
mound they could see for miles. A mile to the west was
the only place where the view was obstructed by the dense
timber along the swampy area around Big Dry Wood
River.

Schell was becoming increasingly certain that someone
didn't want him here. Then there was the last letter he
received from his father dated three years earlier. For per-

haps the hundredth time, he took the worn, folded paper from his knapsack to read.

*Campbell's Hump*
*July 26, 1863*

*My Dear Son,*

*I trust you are as well as when we received your last letter six months ago. Your mother, brothers, and I are as well as can be expected considering our harsh conditions. I am sorry to tell you that the Lord took your sister Elizabeth last month. She had been ailing for some weeks, but with no doctors or medicines since the war, there was little we could do for her. We buried her behind the lookout rock you and she used to play on. I am happy to tell you, however, that baby Martha is a fine little lady now and is beginning to help her mother with the work. We all send our regards.*

*There is much trouble hereabouts. Almost weekly some band of bushwhackers and even regular-army men of both sides range through the country taking what they want. Ray and Tommy take turns keeping watch from our lookout. When they spot any horsemen, your mother and the little ones hide in one of the pits we dug for such purposes. There has been no real law since General Price came through here after the battle at Dry Wood. All our hay and grain has been taken by the armies, first the Confederates and then the Federals. Then in between them there are the Jayhawkers, now bolder than ever, always on the alert for anything to steal or burn. So far we have escaped with losing only stock and crops. We've tried hiding our corn after harvest, but last year some men rode their horses over the field, battering down the corn so that with great labor we could save only a small portion of the crop. This year we had no seed to plant.*

*Our last horse was taken back in May when Federal Captain Anderson Morton rode over from Cedar County and burned Nevada City. I was unfortunate enough to be in town that day. The soldiers took old Charlie, made me give them my last gun, and the money I had with me which was to buy our supplies. Then when the guards weren't looking, I fled for my life. The soldiers were so busy looting and making everyone get out of their homes, so they could burn them down, that they didn't pay attention to an old man like me.*

*The greatest burden for me is that these troops that burned Nevada City and devastated the area were* our *troops, raiding and killing their own citizens. They treat us as if Missouri left the Union, considering everyone in the county their enemies. I yelled out that I was a Union man and had a son in the Union Army fighting in Virginia, but they didn't believe me.*

*This is dangerous country, but I hesitate to burden you with our troubles knowing the danger facing you daily. I tell you only to prepare you when, God willing, you do return.*

*With no newspapers, mail, or any of the services of civilized life, we get only scattered accounts or rumors of what is happening in the rest of the world. I don't even know whether this letter will get out or* not. I will send it with our good neighbors, the McFalls. Their family and ours are the only ones left in this whole area. You may remember the McFalls who live west of us on Big Dry Wood River. They will take this letter on their next trip to sell their furs at Ft. Scott. Business across the border in Kansas is almost normal.

Since I am uncertain what may happen here, I have put all our money and some bonds in the bank in St. Louis for safekeeping until after the war. We will live on what we can raise and subsist on the land just as the McFalls have been doing for some years. Hoping that one of us will survive this hell, I have added your name to the account. When you return, the funds will be there. As you come through St. Louis, make arrangements to get the money so that you, I, and your brothers can develop this ranch the way we envisioned when we came here ten years ago.

I believe in this country as much as always. Isolated as we are, and with our hide-outs, your mother and I believe that we can protect ourselves and our land better here on Campbell's Hump than by moving away as most of the other settlers have done. We will endeavor to stay here and save it for our future.

I am your devoted father. May you keep safe and return when this horror is finished. I pray to the Good Lord above to end this war and bring you safely home to us.

                                    *Samuel E. Campbell*


Schell wiped away the tears that filled his eyes when he read his father's scrawled signature, once strong and bold, but in this letter, faint and trembly.

And that was three years ago! What would he find? From his seat on the creek bank, he scanned the mound again for evidence of buildings or life. Nothing.

When the war began, he was in college in New York. Instead of returning home, he enlisted in a New York regiment with his college friends. His father believed it would be unwise to return to the predominately pro-Confederate Vernon County. Their border county had experienced several years of trouble with Jayhawkers; raids by both Missourians and Kansans back and forth across the state border during the political struggle of granting Kansas statehood. Even before the war between the states, there were incidents, raids, murders, and rape in the borderland where the Campbells settled. Because of the ferocity of some Free-Soilers, like John Brown, many border Missourians sympathized with the Confederacy. Samuel Campbell, a strong supporter of the Union, thought it dangerous for Schell to return home until all was settled.

Schell counted up the years since he was last home. Six years! Little Ray and Tommy would be almost grown by now. And Elizabeth! Little sister who adored him, threw her arms around him when he left those years ago and whispered fearfully, "After you go to college will you still be my brother?"

"I'll always be your brother, forever and ever," he had assured her. Now at his homecoming he could only visit her grave; their playhouse a cemetery, his little brothers sentinels before they had a chance to play.

Finally the nightmare of war ended. As he had traveled west from New York, he noticed everywhere he went people were already living normal lives and forgetting and forgiving the hatreds of the war years. But the moment he stepped off the train at Independence, he sensed the difference. The war here was not over. Riding with Walking Owl through the country, seeing the devastation, Schell Campbell realized just what a toll this area had taken.

But everything was not black, Schell knew. Good things had happened, like escaping the prairie fire and joining up with Walker. He smiled as he glanced at the Osage.

"This is rich country," Walking Owl said.

"The best," Schell agreed.

Walking Owl was leaning his long body against a willow. Under a pile of logs and branches he noticed a muskrat hole. On the opposite bank he saw recent sign of beaver—sapling stumps gnawed to a point like a huge, clumsily sharpened pencils.

Their fright forgotten, the thirsty cattle carefully picked their way back down the steep, black dirt bank, muddying the water. With each step their hooves sunk into the soft mud and splatted as they lifted them from the gooey bottom. Ignoring the brown color of the still water, they drank, squished through the mud to return up the steep bank, knocking still more rich dirt into the water, and corralled by Harris, began to graze on the new grass.

"And your family owns all this?" Walking Owl waved his arm south toward the mound and circled it to encompass the surrounding area.

"Yeah, four tracts, over two thousand acres."

"And there is still land available?"

"Yeah. Last I knew there was good prairie land west of us beyond Big Dry Wood River. I think that this combination of the river timber and the open area would suit you."

Walking Owl's hopeful smile smoothed out the creases

in his forehead. His mission schooling, the many books he was always reading, and his army life had all convinced him that the Osage way of life was no longer possible. His eagerness as he drew closer to his childhood homelands had given his grave face a younger look, belying the gray streaks in his short-cropped, black hair.

"Rich country," he repeated. "With enough of this land a man could combine the best of the Osage and White ways of life."

"You bet." Schell's blue eyes scanned the scene with pride.

"After I revisit my Blue Mounds . . ." Walking Owl did not finish his thought.

"Come on," Schell urged, jumping up quickly. "Let's get going. The cattle should be rested enough now. Two hours should get this herd into the corral on top of The Hump." Cheerful again, he yelled at the dog and cattle. "Yie-e-e, yie-e-e!" he called. "Not far now." Reluctantly the cattle raised their heads from the grass and plodded slowly southward.

Still seeing no silhouette of a house on the mound Schell asked, "Can you handle the herd alone? I'll ride on ahead."

"Sure," Walking Owl said. "Go on. Ole Harris here and me, we can handle them."

Schell loped across the rolling prairie, rounding the base of the mound to find the trail that circled up it. By now he knew there was nobody there. With dread he galloped Solomon over the last ridge before reaching the level area on top to see . . .

Nothing. No house, no barn, no corral. Nothing. Only the young trees he'd seen from the distance, elms, cotton-woods, and locust, about twenty feet high. Cedars, blackberry briars and other brush covered the garden plot. From the top he looked down onto the fields where he and his father had so laboriously plowed under the prairie sod. Instead of neat rows of corn, there were young cedars, elms, cottonwoods, vines, and briars.

Vaulting from his horse, he ran to the house area. There lay a pile of rocks from the chimney, some broken crocks, and charred boards. Where the barn once stood he found bits of metal from harnesses and some bent and blackened horse shoes. Piles of rotted, fire-damaged hay was littered with stalks from last summer's weeds. A new year's growth of green was beginning to carpet the barn lot.

All gone!

His family? Where did they go? He'd heard about the infamous Order Number 11 of August 1863, when a federal general ordered everyone out of the border counties. Is that what happened to his family? Were they moved out? If so, they would have come back. That order was almost three years ago—soon after his father wrote his last letter.

Was it bushwhackers? Jayhawkers?

How could he find out?

The grave. His father's letter told where he had buried Elizabeth. Schell raced to the lookout rock, his first glance confirming his greatest fear. There were, he counted them, one, two, three, four grave mounds neatly laid side by side. The vegetation growth showed they had been there about two years. Beside them was a fallen wooden board on an older grave. He read scratched into the surface, ELIZABETH CAMPBELL, 1863.

Though he clawed in the weeds and brush on the other graves, he could find no markers. Five graves. The older grave was Elizabeth's. But Mother, Father, Ray, Tommy, and Martha. That's a total of six. His gloom lifted for a moment. Who was still alive! Where?

Schell didn't have time to investigate further as he heard Walking Owl's shrill commands, Harris's barks, and the hoof beats and lowing of the cattle as they rounded the turn in the trail that topped the mound.

Suddenly, shots and angry shouts erupted from the opposite, western slope of the mound. Instinctively, both men grabbed their rifles and dived behind the lookout rock.

The first spatter of gunshot ricocheted off the rock, frightening the cattle that started to bolt. But, circling them like a possessed dog, Harris drove them in a compact herd out of range back down the eastern slope.

"Git them cattle outta this country!" came a high-pitched voice.

Covered by the rapid shotgun fire of two boyish riders behind him, a slim, young frontiersman rode at the top speed of his pinto. His homemade wool coat swung loosely on his body as he expertly guided his pony from tree to tree, keeping out of rifle range.

The two veteran soldiers, seeing the youthfulness of their attackers, stood up cautiously to speak to them.

"Wait a minute, young man, these . . ."

Pulling to an abrupt stop and pointing his Sharps rifle at Schell's chest, the slim leader repeated his order, "Git them cattle outta here. If we can't burn you out, we'll shoot you out. Turn 'em 'round and take 'em back to Texas. We won't have no diseased cattle here."

Schell and Walking Owl exchanged astonished glances. Walking Owl crouched. "What the . . ." Schell started to ask.

"Now!" the youth screamed. "Git off this hill." He put a shot into the elm just inches above the place where Schell's head disappeared and another in rapid fire in the rock behind which Walking Owl dropped.

## Chapter Two

Lying prone on his stomach, protected temporarily by the low flat rock, Walking Owl slithered to the far end of the shelf and aimed his Spencer toward the youth who was darting back and forth on his pony. Before shooting he glanced at Schell who was also looking down his sights at the elusive rider. The men caught each other's puzzled glances for a second, long enough for Schell to shake his head to advise caution.

"I mean it," the youth yelled and shot two more bullets at the rock.

Walking Owl backed down the slope where, hidden by the brush, and crouched out of the youth's view and range, he ran to the herd, his tan clothes disappearing among the reds, tans, and roan of the animals. Schell held his place, ready to protect his land and property. Grief for his family boiled up at sight of these riders. Was this how his family died, bushwhacked by young outlaws? Without the protection of the lookout rock, both he and Walking Owl would have been killed. What chance did his aged parents

and little brothers have when he and Walker, two war survivors, almost got killed.

Trained to see everything at once—Walking Owl safely
reaching the herd as well as every movement of the
youth—Schell also scanned the hilltop for the two other
riders. Though young, they certainly were good at ambushing. Being at home again at long last and then finding
the graves of his family had caused him to let down his
guard. Stupid. Even Walking Owl had relaxed his constant
wariness. Those fellows were good. In spite of his danger,
he admired the trio who had so successfully entrapped him.

Where are the other boys? As if in answer he heard one
of them shouting from the direction of the herd. "Hey,
D. C.! These don't look like no Texas cattle. They're
stocky and short-horned."

D. C. spun his horse around rapidly, circling the hilltop
to keep out of range of Schell's rifle, and loped down the
eastern slope. Watching the two boys so intently, Schell
did not hear the third boy.

"Don't you move, soldier," commanded an adolescent
voice behind him. "Don't you move a muscle or I'll fill
you full of shot as sure as I've got you in my sights." Then
he yelled to his companion, "D. C. I've got this one covered."

"Hold him," D. C. yelled back. "Where's the tall one?"

"He ain't here."

Schell laid down his rifle and turned to see his captor.
As he shifted his position, he scanned the slope where only
moments before Walking Owl had faded into the landscape. Harris was barking frantically, circling the cattle to
keep them from bolting and protecting his charges from
these intruders.

After glancing briefly at the cattle, D. C. whistled. Both riders retreated to cover. Almost magically, D. C. appeared beside Schell's captor. "Git up there and keep a lookout fer that other feller," he ordered.

The boy disappeared.

"Them ain't no Texas cattle," D. C. said to Schell, showing relief but not letting down his guard. "So I reckon they ain't diseased. But you've still got to git off this land." When Schell opened his mouth to explain, D. C. said. "I won't listen to yer lies. Take that mutt and them cattle and yer Yankee self and leave."

"I am . . ." Schell started to say.

"Shut up your mouth. Git goin'." Though never letting Schell out of his rifle sights, D. C. took quick glances around. "The other feller?" he demanded, squeezing down on the trigger. Under his wide-brimmed hat pulled down low on his forehead, his eyebrows lowered in determination. "I'd jest as soon shoot you as not. Where's he at?"

"Here." Walking Owl was upon D. C., knocking down his rifle which fired harmlessly into the ground. Schell regained his own weapon and swung around with just enough time to fire a warning at one of the boys. The bullet hit the ground behind the youth as he fled on his pony, disappearing down the western slope. The crashing in the brush told him that the other boy was likewise fleeing.

D. C. struggled in Walking Owl's grip. Though there seemed to be no contest with the slight youth against the tall and muscled Osage, D. C. squirmed out of Walking Owl's grasp. With the quickness of youth, he rolled over several times, regained his feet, and dodging both of the older men's efforts to stop him, raced zigzag among the few trees and brushes to his pony. He leap-frogged into the saddle and disappeared over the western ridge before the men could reach their mounts.

"Follow them," Schell yelled unnecessarily as Walking Owl was already riding down the trackless, grassy western slope. Before seeing to the herd, Schell rode to the ridge. There were no fleeing riders! Though he could see all the way across the prairie to the timber along the river, there was no one but the Osage, who was studying the ground and slowly tracking the horses. When Walking Owl reached the wooded area, he paused.

*He won't enter that*, Schell decided. That almost impenetrable forest, like an island in the open prairie, was caused by two waterways flowing about a half mile apart for a mile or so, creating a swampy, undesirable tract.

As Schell figured, Walking Owl returned to Campbell's Hump after studying the area.

The next few days the men were busy getting settled, making a temporary camp for themselves and a corral for the horses and mules. The first priority before turning the stock out was to brand the cattle with the Campbell brand, a large C under a hill.

Then they turned the cattle loose on the hundreds of grassy acres surrounding The Hump. On the trek down from Independence, some of the cows had calved. More calves came every day. The herd would thrive on the nutritious grasses with only occasional supervision.

The next task for the pair was to plant a garden. Walking Owl cleared the brush from the old plot while Schell fashioned temporary handles for his father's walking plow he'd dug out of the barn ashes. Using one of the mules, they turned the soil, smoothed down the soft, loamy dirt with an improvised log drag, and planted the seed Schell had brought from New York.

That done, they turned their attention to building some permanent shelter. Anticipating Cynthia's arrival in a few weeks, Schell decided to build one good room out of the logs he and Walking Owl could cut along Dry Wood River. Later when he had time to ride to one of the towns for lumber, and after Cynthia came, he could add more rooms to replace the home he had described to his eastern bride-to-be—the fine house overlooking the miles of Campbell land. The view and the land were still there; the house he could replace.

The two men spent several days cutting logs and dragging them back the mile across the prairie with the mules. They were not ambushed; the cattle grazed uninterrupted; there were no new prairie fires.

"Good setup." From the building site, Walking Owl waved his hand in a circle to encompass the area around The Hump. At any time from the top of the mound, the men could see the cattle. No need to go riding over the prairie searching for the herd, for it never roamed beyond the two- or three-mile range within view of the house. The animals had everything they needed—unlimited grass, water in the draws from the spring rains and the nearby river, and the salt the men put out for them. Walking Owl clicked his tongue in approval.

"Yeah," Schell smiled. "We can keep track of them from up here better than down there." He gazed out over the prairie which appeared flat from The Hump, though in reality the land was gently rolling with draws and depressions that could hide cattle when searching for them below.

"Cynthia will soon be here," he said dreamily, stroking his beard. "Then it will be better."

Walking Owl glanced at Schell. "It's still pretty raw out here. Reckon she'll take to it?"

"She'll love it just as I do." When the Osage shrugged his shoulders, Schell said, "Since we've had no more trouble from the fellows that ambushed us that first day, I figure that they rode in here from Kansas."

Walking Owl shook his head. "No, they're living in the river bottom."

Schell stopped working to stare at him. "Are you sure?"

"Yeah. I've seen their tracks. Besides the three we saw, there's a woman and a girl."

"You've seen them?" Schell asked in amazement.

"Not the women. One or the other of the boys watches us when we cut wood. Since they haven't tried to jump us, I just kept track of them, letting on that I didn't see them."

"You knew this all the time?" Schell's admiration of Walking Owl's ability was mixed with exasperation at his lack of communication.

"Yeah. I figured they were just scared about the Texas cattle fever. I heard about it in Westport and Independence."

"What's that all about?"

"Well see, since the end of the war some Texas cattle drovers have brought herds to Missouri to the end of the railroad to sell—looking for a market for all their cattle they couldn't sell during the war. Now Texas cattle don't get the fever, immune against it, I reckon, but the Missouri cattle aren't immune." Walking Owl stopped.

"So local cattle catch the fever and die?" Schell asked.

Walking Owl nodded. "Along the Missouri border, men barricade the area, forcing the herds back."

"And that is what these fellows were doing with setting the fire and ambushing us?"

Walking Owl nodded again.

Schell thought for a moment. "You say these boys are *always* watching us when we get logs?"

"Yeah. I think that they live back in that swampy area between the river and creek. The tracks all lead back that way."

"Maybe we ought to pay them a visit—neighborly like."

"And get shot full of lead, more than likely."

"Well, they don't seem to be hostile now. We haven't heard anything more from them the week we've been here." Schell picked up his axe and resumed chopping. His muscles rippled on his bare arms, already tanned from the spring sun.

In spite of his weariness, Schell had trouble sleeping that night, but not because of the possibility of another ambush. For several days he and Walking Owl had taken turns keeping watch, but they stopped after a few days with no renewal of hostilities and with Harris alert to warn them. What worried him was his future here. Perhaps he should check at Nevada City to see if the land title was in order. He had heard stories about land jumpers seizing the titles, or corrupt officials falsifying the records. Maybe the records were all destroyed when the town was burned? He must go to town to check as soon as possible.

He worried too that he wouldn't have time to prepare for his New York fiancée's coming in the summer. He hadn't missed Walking Owl's negative reaction when he talked about Cynthia's arrival. Neither he nor she had anticipated that everything would be burned. That his family . . .

Schell never ceased thinking about his family lying there in the graveyard. What had happened to them? Who survived and where was he (or she)? Only Walking Owl's wise advice that he should first get the ranch working kept him from riding off half-cocked to find out what happened. "Their deaths were over two years ago," his friend had told him. "A few more weeks won't hurt. You must first take care of your cattle and ranch."

The next morning after they had hauled to the old house site on the mound the last of the logs they needed to build the one room, Walking Owl tapped Schell on the shoulder and pointed to the edge of the level area. Mounted on their ponies, about fifteen feet apart, each with his gun pointed toward the building site, sat the three youths.

Walking Owl pressed Schell's shoulder warning him to do nothing. Taking his cue from the Osage, Schell put down his axe, and took a step toward D. C. who was in the middle. Blaming himself that he hadn't kept a better watch, he held out his hand and started to speak.

"Don't you come one step farther," D. C. ordered, his eyes flashing in anger under his hat brim, his rifle pointed at Schell. His brothers leveled their shotguns at Walking Owl.

Schell halted. "I understand we are neighbors and you live between the river and creek down in the bottom. You don't intend to shoot us or you would have killed us any one of the days that you watched us cut logs."

D. C.'s mouth opened, his gun wavered just a second. His brothers both stared at Schell in amazement, momentarily letting the Osage out of their vision. When they looked back, Walking Owl was gone. Flustered, the boys looked at D. C. for orders. Though D. C.'s eyes squinted in anger at the boys' incompetence, they never left his gun sights that were on Schell's chest.

"Don't be concerned, fellows," Schell said. "My friend won't shoot you. Just as you could have shot us anytime, so could he have shot you. We are neighbors, so let's not fight."

"No, we ain't neighbors. You got no right to be here. We've come to tell you one last time to git off this land. It ain't yours. You can't come sashayin' in here after we've kept it from the Rebs and the Yanks, the Jayhawkers, and all the other trash that's been here. And now you Yankee soldiers think you can jest come in here and take over what don't belong to you."

D. C.'s voice raised higher and higher as he spoke until it was almost a scream. "This here is *Campbell* land, legal and free. You got to git. This is our last warnin'. Next time we'll shoot to kill."

The three youths put shots all around Schell and in the sumac brush where Walking Owl had disappeared. They turned their ponies and galloped toward the western slope, disappearing over the ridge.

Schell started to follow them, but reappearing beside him, Walking Owl once again put his restraining hand on his shoulder. "Let them go. They don't aim to hurt us now. I'll find out where they live, and we can pay a visit to the woman, who's probably their mother."

Unconvinced, Schell still tried to follow the youths. "Their leader said *Campbell land*. Did you hear him?"

"Yeah."

"Then they know about my family! Somehow they are

protecting this land." He grabbed his friend's hand. "Walker, maybe one of them is . . ." He paused a moment, his excitement fading. "No, none of them was Tommy or Ray. My brothers were big enough when I left that I'd still recognize them, and they'd surely know me, even with this beard." He tried to picture details of the attackers, but dressed in their shapeless, homemade clothes and wearing hats pulled down to their eyes, he couldn't remember any features other than D. C.'s flashing blue eyes.

"They must be the McFalls that my father wrote about."

"Most likely," Walking Owl agreed.

"Then they'll know what happened here." Schell motioned toward the graveyard. "All I have to do is tell them who I am." Schell started once again toward the west.

"Hold on a minute. Let's think this out. That leader won't let you talk. He'll likely shoot you as he warned he would."

"You're right." Schell sat down on one of the logs.

"Next time we meet it should be on *our* terms," Walking Owl said. "They obviously never considered that you might be a Campbell."

"I wonder why not."

Schell picked up his axe to resume his work. His companion stared at the blind western side of the mound, thinking.

"Let's pay their mother a call later on when *we* decide," he said, "sometime when they are all together."

"Good idea. I'll need to bring some proof of who I am. That D. C. acted like he was protecting this land, not for himself but for someone else—maybe my father? Mother? One of the boys?" Once again Schell grabbed his friend's arm, his voice unnaturally high and trembly. "Walker, I *have* to find out."

"Okay, okay." Walking Owl patted Schell's shoulder, calming him down. "But be patient just a little more. You've waited six years. Give me a couple of days to check them out. I'll need to do it at night when they stop spying on us." He picked up his axe. "Now, let's get to work on this house of yours. The sooner we get it done and settle this matter with these McFalls, the sooner we can go to my old territory over at Blue Mounds."

Schell could not remember Walking Owl giving such a long speech. He knew it was good advice. And at the same time Walking Owl subtly reminded Schell of his obligation in return for all his friend had done. Willing himself to be patient, and more optimistic than he had been since he found the five graves, Schell swung his axe at the next log.

Working hard on the cabin, Schell was able to pass the next few days. An hour before dusk of the third day, without once mentioning the subject beforehand, Walking Owl said, "Walk the long route and circle around to the timber edge until you get to where that trail fords Dry Wood River. Do you remember it?"

"Yes, I know the place."

"Don't let them see you. I'll meet you there and we'll go together. We won't take the horses. I'll tie Harris here to the tree by the fire so they'll think we're still here."

"You found their house?" Schell was amazed though he should have been accustomed by now to Walking Owl's reticence.

"Yeah. Pretty clever they are. Well hidden—on stilts above high water in the big trees surrounded by marshy land. We'll have to wade. They'll all be there eating supper when we get there."

Schell loaded his Smith & Wesson pistol, strapped on his officer's holster, changed into a darker shirt, and pulled his hat down to his eyes before descending the southern slope of The Hump out of view of the McFalls. While walking cautiously to reach their meeting place, he marvelled that only three weeks had passed since he met Walking Owl. In that short time he had come to admire him and trust him completely. Numerous times his knowledge and friendship had made the journey and work here at home possible. Schell hoped that when the time came to reciprocate on the Osage's behalf that he could be of as much help. He wasn't clear just what he was supposed to do—accompanying his friend to honor his ancestral grounds and something about retrieving what his father left there.

Schell knew that one of the reasons Walking Owl needed him was to have a White man there to verify and legalize anything they did. Off of their reservations, Indians had no rights to property and few other rights. Well, if his presence at Blue Mounds helped Walking Owl, then he would be glad to be there.

Strange, though. Schell rarely thought of Walker as an Osage, except in situations like this one tonight. No White man that Schell ever knew had the observational and deductive skills and the knowledge of the land that his friend possessed. When he did remember he was an Indian, it was in admiration of his non-White abilities.

However, Schell himself was no amateur at these arts. Being raised on this land and experiencing the raids and night watches of the army had taught him much. He didn't doubt that the two of them could outsmart D. C., though he admitted he respected the ability of that shrewd youth and his wily brothers.

How this timbered area brought back his childhood! Then Schell had known every part of it. Relying on his memory, since in getting the logs they had cut only along the timber's edge, he soon reached the meeting place. Resting on a mossy ledge overlooking the muddy waters of the river, even with the disappearing light, he could still make out the once familiar landmarks. Here the river spread out over some exposed rocks, making a natural ford. The usual steep mud banks gave way to a gradual incline to the water, allowing wagons to cross. Schell wondered if this was where Confederate General Price had crossed on his flight back to Arkansas after his defeat at Westport. Likely, as there were very few natural fords such as this.

The muddy water looked almost clear in the dwindling light as it flowed over the rock shelf, falling into the ditch-like trench of mud banks as the river continued its way north. The early May breeze was warm. Tree frogs chirped and some birds called. Schell heard the mournful call of the hoot owl.

So tranquil. After years of danger, the peacefulness tried to disarm him, but he wasn't deceived. There was no real peace yet. This mission tonight was full of danger. Up on The Hump, the McFalls had demonstrated that they wouldn't shoot to kill, but down here? Penetrating their sanctuary was another matter. If he and Walking Owl fouled up, they'd be killed. The fury and hate in D. C.'s eyes left him no doubt.

Walking Owl appeared and beckoned him to follow him

along a route that required the least wading through the marshy soil. Though the night was mild, before they reached higher ground around the McFall house, they were chilled from the cold water seeping through their boots. A gray dog blocked their path. His low, menacing growl died in his throat even before Walking Owl tossed him some meat. Wagging his tail, he came up to the Osage who patted his head and spoke softly to him. In the same manner the men passed two more hounds that let them approach the building without barking a warning.

The men reached the clearing and were within a few yards of the house before they spied any evidence of habitation—a light from a shuttered window flickering faintly through the brush and trees. What resourcefulness! Schell respected not only the McFalls, but also Walking Owl for finding the family that had eluded both armies and numerous outlaws. Walking Owl crept to the steps to the back door, signaling Schell to position himself on the porch by the front door.

Inside, around a table lit by two candles, sat five people. D. C. faced the front door, one brother was on the left, and the other had his back to the door. On the right was a woman dressed in a faded and patched homespun wool dress. She appeared old, but from her brown hair and alert, lean body, Schell decided she was probably not over forty-five. Next to her was a girl about ten or eleven dressed in trousers like the boys. Her dark hair was in long braids down her back.

Waiting for Walking Owl's signal, Schell studied D. C.. Relaxed now, smiling at his mother, he seemed younger than before. Maybe it was because he wasn't wearing his broad-brimmed hat which had hidden his short, reddish-brown hair. However, the shadows cast from the candles gave his thin, pale face a maturity that belied his slim build.

At the exact moment that Walking Owl slipped noiselessly through the back door, Schell stepped into the room. Seeing Schell, D. C. started to rise, as did the brother facing the back door who spotted the Osage at the same time. Knowing from his previous scouting trips where they kept their guns, Walking Owl grabbed them before those at the table fully comprehended what was happening.

Schell did not draw his pistol that was clearly visible to all but the boy with his back to him.

"Don't be alarmed, Mrs. McFall," Schell said with his best New York manners. "Please pardon our abrupt intrusion into your home, but we need to talk with you."

Mrs. McFall started to rise.

"Please do not get up. I'd like it if you all stayed just where you are." Schell moved over slightly, enough that the boy with his back to him could see him. Walking Owl's six foot, eight inches dominated the room. No one else moved.

"I am happy to make your acquaintance, Mrs. McFall. I've met your sons, though not in the best of circumstances. D. C. here," he pointed to the youth whose face was red with anger and frustration, "D. C. did all the talking without letting me explain."

Mrs. McFall shot a glance at D. C., shaking her head slightly, warning him to take no action and be quiet, that she would handle this. D. C. frowned, bit his lip, but obeyed. *Good*, Schell thought. She can control this fiery son. *So far, so good.*

He continued talking only to her in a pleasant tone as

if on a routine social call. "Mrs. McFall, I want to commend you on holding on here and surviving during all the horrors of the war. Coming down from Independence, my friend," he nodded his head toward Walking Owl, "and I saw much destruction and many graveyards, including the one on Campbell's Hump. Very few people have been able to survive, much less to remain in their homes."

After the initial surprise, followed by fear and anger, the people at the table were beginning to show curiosity.

"But I forget my manners, ma'am. Let me introduce ourselves. This is Walking Owl, grandson of Pawhuska of the Osage Tribe. He served in the Union Army and is now my partner. I am . . ." he paused. Retrieving his father's letter from his inner pocket, he opened it and held it out to the woman. "Because I was afraid that you would not believe me, to prove who I am, I'm showing you this letter, the last one I received from my father."

Mrs. McFall took the letter, glanced at it briefly as those do who can't read and handed it back.

"Does anyone here know how to read?" Schell asked.

No one answered. This was a problem Schell hadn't anticipated. "Well, as I said, this was the last letter I received from my father. I am Schell Campbell." Schell ignored the murmurings and shufflings in the room to continue. "My father is Samuel Campbell. As soon as I was released from the hospital, where I spent several months after the war was over recuperating from the prison at Andersonville, and when I recovered my strength, I journeyed back to Campbell's Hump to rejoin my family, only to find that they must be dead. I found five graves."

The atmosphere in the room was explosive. The woman and the younger brothers stared at him in disbelief. D. C.

jumped up in anger, "He's a liar. The letter is a fake. It's jest another trick to git the ranch." Furious, he started toward Schell. Walking Owl's strong hand on his shoulder, pushed him back into his seat.

The brothers clamored, echoing D. C.'s words. The girl was crying, big sobs shaking her small body. The mother, even while continuing to hold her sons in check with her stern look, put her arm around the girl, drawing her to her side. "There, there, dearie."

"I can read," the girl said, controlling her sobs. Schell glanced at Mrs. McFall who nodded. He handed the child the letter.

As soon as she glanced at it and read just a few words, she cried, "It's Papa's writing. It's his letter."

"It's a trick," D. C. shouted. "Anyone could git the letter. That don't prove nothin'. Don't you see, these two varmints is jest some more of them scum tryin' to steal yer land, Marthie."

"But this *is* Papa's letter."

"That may be, but you know that yer brother died in the war. Before yer pa was killed, he got the news hisself." D. C. looked at Schell with venom. "This man's lyin'."

## Chapter Three

"**I** don't know how you found us out and how you know our names, but you ain't Schell Campbell," Mrs. McFall said. "We ain't hankerin' to kill you, or we'd a-done it when you first come on The Hump. And it don't look like you plan to kill us, or you'd a-done it instead of bargin' in here with yer lies. But mister-whoever-you-are, it won't work. Schell Campbell is dead."

Schell hardly heard what she was saying for staring at the girl. She had said the letter was her father's, and D. C. called her Marthie. His baby sister! The one who survived? She was barely four years old when he left. The girl, no longer crying stared boldly back at Schell, the letter still in her hand.

"No, Marthie, this ain't Schell," D. C. repeated, looking from the girl to Schell.

Everyone was talking, each trying to be heard over the others. Walking Owl spoke for the first time. "Quiet."

His deep voice dominated the room, as did his presence. Rifle cradled in his arms, his eyes glinting sparks of anger,

36

he left them no doubt that he was an Osage of high rank in spite of his American clothes.

In the sudden silence, he said in his accustomed soft voice, "We came here to talk. Listen to what my friend has to say."

The room was quiet enough to hear a distant bullfrog. All eyes were on Schell.

"I *am* Schell Campbell." He reached into his pocket for another paper which he gave to Martha. "This is my army discharge paper, dated, you see Martha, December 1865."

"That's right," Martha said, looking at Mrs. McFall, hope glowing in her eyes. She read aloud, " 'This is to certify that Schell W. Campbell, First Lieutenant of the Sixth New York Regiment, is hereby Honorably Discharged from the military service of the United States of America.' It says here, 'Date of separation December 11, 1865.' "

"Don't prove nothin'. Papers could be forged," D. C. said.

"It looks real to me," Martha said.

"What does she know?" D. C. appealed to his mother. "She's jest a kid."

"Let the man continue," Mrs. McFall said, glancing briefly at Walking Owl who continued to tower menacingly over them all. Inflexible, D. C. scowled at Schell.

"Yes, papers can be forged," Schell said, still speaking to Mrs. McFall, ignoring D. C.'s interruptions. His business was with the head of the household who was obviously the mother, and with Martha now that he had found her. He ached to run to her, enfold the child in his arms. Giddy with the knowledge that one member of his family survived, he checked himself. First he had to prove himself to these people.

"Yes," he said, "it was possible for someone at the prisons and Federal hospitals to steal papers from dying soldiers and later use them to their advantage. I know it happened. I was there and saw it being done, but these papers are not stolen or forged."

D. C. grunted in disbelief; though silent, Mrs. McFall's compressed lips indicated strong doubt. Martha was hanging on his every word, already convinced.

"Since you don't believe the papers, perhaps I can convince you who I am in other ways." He talked this time to Martha. "Our parents came to The Hump in June of 1853. We came here from Ohio, down the Ohio River, up the Mississippi and the Missouri to Independence, then by wagon over the prairie the rest of the way to Nevada City where they looked for land. When they saw our Hump rising all alone overlooking the prairie, they knew that was the place they were searching for."

He turned to the woman, "As you may recall, Mrs. McFall, because you and your husband were one of the first settlers in the county, the 1850s were boom years for settlement. The county filled up in just a few years. My grandfather, for his service in the War of 1812, was granted warrants for a hundred and sixty acres, redeemable at any land office. He gave them to my father. Then my father bought warrants at a dollar an acre from other veterans in Ohio who didn't want to move east. As head of the household, he entered for a quarter section on his own. So when he arrived at Nevada City, he could lay title to a thousand acres. Later, after we settled here, he bought more land. When I left for college six years ago, he owned four sections—two thousand, five hundred and sixty acres, with The Hump near the center."

Martha's shining eyes never left his face.

"Am I right, so far?" Schell asked Mrs. McFall.

"Yes," she admitted unwillingly, her lips less tightly shut.

"He coulda found all that out easy enough," D. C. said.

Ignoring him, Schell continued, "I was thirteen when we came. Elizabeth was ten, my brothers, Tommy and Ray, were five and four. Martha, you were born in the new house just after we moved out of our first cabin. I remember my father working hard to get the big house finished. He didn't want one of his children born in a log shanty. That was 1856."

"Papa told me that lots of times," Martha said.

"Mrs. McFall, I remember that you and your husband trapped along the river. Our families didn't associate with each other much because our affairs led us in different directions. I do remember that you had some children, boys and a girl, I think. I remember one time a girl about a year or two younger than me beat me in a foot race at some gathering at Deerfield."

The two younger brothers snickered and exchanged glances. Mrs. McFall was observing Schell carefully.

"Go on," Mrs. McFall said. Her lightly clamped lips relaxed. Her hands unclenched. Absorbing every word, Martha left the table to stand beside Schell. A faint smile began to warm her pale, thin face as she looked into his eyes.

"Well, let's see. Maybe I should explain why I took so long to return after the war."

"Yeah, all the *real* soldiers come home last year," D. C. sneered.

Ignoring him, Schell asked Martha. "When was the last letter you got from me—uh, from Schell?"

"Two years ago."

"Do you remember the date?"

"Of course, Mama and Papa read it over and over. It was May 1864. You wrote that you were with General Grant in Virginia near Richmond, trying to wear down Lee's Army."

"Ah! Then you didn't know that I was wounded the next month. Before my unit could get back to the field to get me and the other wounded men, a Confederate patrol picked us up and sent us to their prison camp at Andersonville in Georgia."

"Schell's Colonel wrote his pa that he was killed June 3, 1864, in Virginia fightin' Lee in the Battle at Cold Harbor," the woman said.

"No, not killed. I was there, but I wasn't killed. I can see why my regiment thought so. Our side had over seven thousand casualties in that battle. How could anyone keep track of that many individual men? Probably when I was missing, my colonel assumed I was dead. I almost was. That night in a tent on the outskirts of the Confederate Army camp, somebody removed the minié-ball and sewed me up. The next day, wagon loads of us were taken to Andersonville Prison. I thought I would die on the trip, and at the prison, for several weeks I was sick enough that I wished I had died. Thousands did die, not so much from their wounds, but from typhoid and other diseases."

"Where was the wound?" D. C. asked. His voice was less belligerent.

"In the shoulder."

"Show us," he demanded.

Schell removed his coat, unbuttoned his shirt and long underwear down to his waist and folded them back to expose his left shoulder. Across his shoulder and almost reaching his neck was an ugly, jagged scar, still bluish-red in a few spots.

Martha caught her breath. "Does it hurt?"

"Not much. At night after swinging the axe all day, it is sore." He flexed his muscles, moving his arm to show there was some soreness. Then he buttoned back his clothes.

Mrs. McFall and the younger boys had lost their wariness. "Let me ask you jest one question to prove who you are."

"Sure."

"What was the pet name that yer father called yer mother?" Mrs. McFall asked.

Schell smiled. "Mousy." The McFalls, including D. C., gasped. "He called her 'Mousy,' because she was the only one in the family that didn't have the black Irish hair and blue eyes like Martha and I have. Before it turned white, her hair was a dull brown-black and her eyes were gray."

"Well, I guess you are Schell Campbell." Smiling Mrs. McFall stood up and held out her hand. "Welcome back and excuse our treatin' you so rough, but we can't trust nobody. We've been a-tryin' to keep anyone from stealin' Campbell's Hump from Marthie, here. We've already run off some trash out to take what they can git."

"It seems that I am the one in your debt, Mrs. McFall."

"Ruby," she corrected him. "Call me Ruby."

"Yes, I remember. Your husband was called Mac."

"And this here bigger boy is Red and the other is Buddy. I see you already know D. C.'s name."

Schell shook hands with the younger brothers, who smiled. When he held out his hand to D. C., the youth stared straight at him, not hostile as before, but not ready yet to shake his hand.

"And this is my little Martha." He pulled the child to him, hugging her. She put her thin arms around him as if she would never let him go. "Do you remember me, Martha?"

"Yes. We talked about you all the time after you left. We kept your picture until it got burned with the house. But I couldn't remember exactly what you looked like. You didn't have a beard and mustache then. You're thinner and not as tall as I remembered."

Schell laughed. "That's because you are bigger now." Turning to Ruby he said, "I am in your debt for all you have done for my family and especially Martha. And what about your family? Your husband? He's . . ."

Ruby nodded, motioning westward beyond the marsh. "We also have a cemetery. Three graves."

"Your husband and . . ."

"Two children, a boy and a girl."

"I wondered about the girl I remembered," Schell said.

One of the boys snickered. D. C. shook his head at him.

Ruby invited the men to join them in supper, "It's a poor celebration for yer homecomin', but all we got to give."

Martha got two more plates and pulled up a couple of stools.

During the meal and afterwards the McFalls and Martha told Schell what happened after his father's last letter—

what they experienced and saw and what they later pieced together from the evidence.

Even before Nevada City was burned, the Campbell and McFall families, being the only ones left for miles around, joined forces for mutual help and protection. Ruby and Mac felt safe living in the lowlands between the river and creek. Their home had not been noticed throughout the Jayhawker troubles before the war. Nor at the beginning of the war in 1861 did the Confederate soldiers find their home, horses, and other stores after the skirmish at Big Dry Wood near Deerfield, a village six miles north, down the river from them. General Price had retreated with his army to Arkansas on the open prairie, living off the land as he went. The main body of his army even used the natural ford to cross the river without detecting the McFall house less than a mile away.

Determined to stay with their land, the McFalls' strategy was to conceal their presence, but be prepared should anyone discover their house. To that end they made the small log house blend into the environment by letting the clearing grow up in brush and weeds, erasing their paths in the woods, and keeping the stock in various other equally concealed locations. They escaped notice by shuttering the windows and keeping fires to a minimum.

Then to protect themselves should they be discovered, they trained the children to keep watch and warn of any strangers, using a series of bird calls for different contingencies. With the first warning, Ruby, or whoever was in the house, would put out the fire and post herself at a window with the always-ready guns. Other members of the family within earshot of the warnings would position themselves at designated spots.

Taking advantage of their natural cover and using their own ingenuity, the McFalls escaped detection from the marauding armies and local bushwhackers.

The Campbells' situation was different. Perched atop the hill, in plain view for miles around, sat the big Campbell house. Since concealment was impossible, the Campbells relied on defense. Mac McFall had tried to persuade them to move to the river bottom or some other more protected location until the danger was over. But like Mac, Sam Campbell was also determined he wouldn't be run off his land. Yes, he agreed, his house was exposed to view, but that was a defensive advantage because they could spot anyone coming from miles away—with plenty time to flee, hide, or repel their attackers. Sam also had a wife as determined as he to remain there and sons able to keep watch.

Just as the McFalls secured their place, so did the Campbells. They believed that if their mound was invaded, their best protection was to hide. Therefore, since there was no cover on the grassy summit, Sam and the boys dug several pits and cave-like hideouts near the house and in various places on and around The Hump. They supported them with logs and covered them with brush or prairie sod to blend into the landscape. Having lost their stock during the first years of the war and the last horse at the burning of Nevada City, they needed to protect and hide only themselves and what food they obtained from hunting, trapping, and gathering in the wild.

The two families used the same bird call signals, and

devised means of warning each other if necessary, as the two homes were less than two miles apart.

The Campbells escaped Order Number 11. In August 1863, believing that borderland Missourians were harboring and protecting Confederate guerrillas, Federal General Thomas Ewing ordered the entire population to leave the Missouri counties on the Kansas border, following up the order with troops that forcibly moved people to military posts prepared for them. Then they burned the vacated buildings. Since Nevada City had already been burned just two months before, the general didn't bother too much with Vernon County. He sent out a few army details to move anyone still there, but they did not ride as far south as The Hump. It was illegal for anyone to remain in the county, and the two families breathed better when the soldiers returned to Kansas City. For several months they stayed close to home.

The next major attack was seven months later. Though never finding the McFalls, small groups of drifters looking for handouts frequently bothered the Campbells. The usual result was that they lost needed supplies. But one dreary, chilly day in March 1864, Tommy Campbell spotted a larger-than-usual group of riders coming toward them from the northeast, from the direction of Nevada City. He gave the warning whistle that many horsemen were coming, and as instructed by his father and Mac, buried himself in the brush beside the lookout rock, where he could observe the strangers' movements without being seen. He cocked his rifle.

His mother and eight-year-old Martha were in the house. They quickly doused the fire, grabbed most of the food they had in the house and ran to the nearest pit shelter.

They always left some food to appease the intruders, hoping they would think that was all there was and leave.

Mrs. Campbell didn't know exactly where her husband and Ray were. They had left earlier to run their rabbit traps. She and Martha worried that they would be caught out on the prairie with no cover.

Tommy whistled again. The riders were closer, and sighting the house on the top of the hill, started up the steep northern face. One of them veered off to the left, circling the mound. When he reached the winding trail that led to the top, he shouted to his companions, who retraced their route for the easier one.

Sam Campbell and his son Ray meanwhile, on the opposite side of the mound, returning from the south with their day's catch, were too far away to hear Tommy's warning whistle, or the horsemen. They were starting up the trail when they heard the rider yell back to his gang. There was no cover on the newly greening March grassland.

"Quick, run," Sam hissed.

Ray bolted across the slope trying to reach a pit on the southern side before being seen. Sam held his ground. Jeering, the rider approached him. When he got within range, Sam leveled his rifle at him, warning him to come no farther. To prove he meant it, he fired a warning shot. The horse reared, knocking the rider to the ground. Sam grabbed the horse, mounted, and galloped toward the river for help. He did not know there were other riders galloping around the foot of the mound.

Within minutes the others reached the scene, angry at the show of defense and infuriated that their leader lost his horse. Three of them chased Sam over the prairie, two went after the fleeing boy, while the rest spread out over The Hump to reach the top from different directions.

From his perch, Tommy frantically whistled the signals to let his mother and Martha know of the assailants' movements.

At the river, alerted by the gunshots, the McFalls made their usual protective preparations. Mac and Red ran to the timber edge just in time to see the three men gain on Sam. Getting within gunshot range, the lead rider fired into Sam's back. Sam fell to the ground, his borrowed horse galloping on toward the woods. One of the bushwhackers circled in front of the runaway mount, grabbed his reins, and loped slowly back to The Hump. Sam lay face down, his blood staining the new spring grass.

At almost the same time there were shots closer to The Hump where the two bushwhackers overtook and shot Ray Campbell. The boy fell. The outlaws circled him before retracing their route to the trail up the hill.

More shots came from the summit. The bushwhackers had approached the top from three sides. Finding no defense, they raced around the buildings, yelling. When the ones who had killed Sam and Ray joined them, including the leader who once again was mounted on his horse, all but two dismounted and tromped through the house and other buildings, taking the scant supplies they found.

Fired up from the killings and angry at not finding more booty, they set fire to all the buildings. The wooden structures blazed up immediately, making a torch that was seen ten miles away in Nevada City. The fire, quickly igniting the carpet of last season's dried grass, spread rapidly to the lookout rock and found the brush hiding Tommy. As he tried to escape, one of the men shouted a warning. Several shots rang out. Tommy fell, his blood running into a hollow place in the rock.

"Bound to be a woman here," the leader said.

"Ain't here unless she's burned up in the fire," another answered laughing.

"Got to be. I seen women's gear in the house," the leader said. "Look for a hidin' place."

The men tramped over every foot of the summit, discovering one pit with some stashed supplies. Jubilantly, they took the food and renewed their search.

Mrs. Campbell and Martha did not know what was happening when Tommy's calls ceased. They heard the shots and intermittent noises from the attackers when one of them came near their pit. As the noise above became pronounced, Mrs. Campbell shoved Martha into a hollow place in the corner and covered her with the leaves and trash that had fallen into the pit. Curled into a ball in the damp hole, Martha obeyed her mother's order to make no noise *no matter what happened.*

A bushwhacker soon discovered the pit. Though Mrs. Campbell fired at them, they wrested the shotgun away from her and pulled her out. They did not notice Martha. Although the child would never tell what happened to her mother, Mrs. Campbell's bruised and gunshot-riddled body told the story.

The bushwhackers loaded up their loot and galloped off. When they disappeared south over the prairie, the McFalls rushed to The Hump to find, of the whole Campbell family, only little Martha alive. They buried the dead beside Elizabeth's grave near the lookout rock and took Martha into their family. The Hump remained untouched until after the war when the young McFalls successfully ran off two would-be squatters.

"Then, Schell," Ruby concluded, "you returned with Walking Owl."

Schell had listened quietly to the story, his arm around Martha, tears streaming down his face. When he could compose himself he asked Ruby gently, "And your husband and children?"

"It was the next fall after yer family's deaths. We almost survived the war. Even then it wasn't rovin' outlaws, bushwhackers, or the armies, but low-down, dirty, deserters who knew this county. One of 'em even ate at our table. See, afore the war he trapped with Mac and the young'uns. He was one of us."

Her face composed, Ruby continued, telling her story without emotion. "Well, after General Price's final defeat at Westport . . . When was that D. C.?"

"October 1864."

"Oh yes. Well, after he was whupped there the second time and this time for good, his army had to git to Arkansas any way they could as fast as they could. They crossed the Marmaton River jest north of Deerfield and camped overnight in Deerfield. They was runnin' hard, leavin' wagons and ammunition as they went. Some of our guns here are ones we found dumped into the Dry Wood River. The boys and D. C. cleaned them up so we could use them.

"In Price's army was some local boys who knowed the country. When the army fled through here, they dropped out and hid until the war was over. Now the army itself passed on by us, never findin' us because they kept to the open land. But jest a few days after the last of the chasin' Federals passed, here comes this feller up to our house as

brave as can be, shouting, 'Mac! Ruby! It's me, Hank Teller.' The one I told you about that used to trap with Mac.

"  'Course, we invited him in. He told all about his stay
in the Confederate Army and how he left. That was his
business, none of ours. We listened politely when all the
time he was sizin' us up. Then a couple of weeks later, he
come back with a gang, not friendly this time, but out to
take what we had. Afore Mac and the young'uns could git
their guns, they shot down Mac and our oldest boy and
girl. The rest of us had time to git our guns and we clipped
four of 'em afore Hank and one other got away. They took
Mac's big sorrel and D. C.'s black, the best horses we
had."

Ruby spoke so matter-of-factly that Schell would have
thought she was speaking of some other family, except for
the pinpoints of hate in her eyes, her clenched hands, and
rigid posture. D. C. and the boys were equally tense, the
fury in their faces even greater than they had shown when
confronting him and Walking Owl.

"We were taken in by a supposed friend that killed three
of us. You can understand why my young'uns mistrusted
you."

"Yes, I can. And Martha witnessed this killing, too?"

Martha was trembling, almost crying.

"Yes, we all did. So as you see there are only four of
us McFalls left and two of you Campbells. Our troubles
ain't over yet. Hank Teller's still on the prowl—holed up
somewhere over the border in Kansas. And he ain't the
only varmint hereabouts. It is worse than during the war,
for then we knowed who our enemy was. Sometimes it
was the Jayhawkers, sometimes the Confederates, and
sometimes the Federals. But it was a war and the sides

was easier to understand. Nowadays anyone new comin' into the country is a possible enemy, and so are former neighbors."

"Not this neighbor," Schell said. "I can never repay my debt to you for taking care of Martha. I'm with you all the way."

"Count me in, too," Walking Owl said. During the entire evening he had said very little. All the time he was watching Ruby and D. C. "I'll help both families. You deserve it and I've decided to settle here."

Ruby looked at him a long time, studying him as he had her. "Good," she smiled at him, "now we have two men and my two almost-grown boys besides D. C. here who is better than most men."

D. C.'s signals to his mother went unnoticed. Red and Buddy snickered again and poked each other.

"What do you mean?" Schell asked. "Granted, D. C. is small, but he's smarter and wilier than most men. He certainly is a man."

Everyone except Schell laughed. Walking Owl was the one to explain. He grinned mischievously as he explained, "Schell, D. C. is a *woman*."

## Chapter Four

"A woman!" Schell blinked his eyes, then opened them wide, staring at D. C.. His mouth gaped.

Everyone else was laughing. Walking Owl clapped his hands on his thighs in fun, greatly enjoying Schell's embarrassment. Red and Buddy, now that the secret was out, laughed loudest of all. Gleefully, Ruby shot a look of admiration at Walking Owl. And D. C., for the first time since Schell had seen him—her—smiled. An impish light came into her eyes, which for the first time Schell noticed were framed by long, upsweeping eyelashes. Infected by the general merriment, she also laughed, displaying small, even teeth.

Schell looked at Martha, who happily nodded agreement.

"How long have you known?" Schell asked Walking Owl.

"I suspected it that first day. But tonight . . . Look at her."

Schell stared at her. D. C. was blushing now, her red

52

face almost the color of her hair. "I never thought . . . Your name . . . I never heard of a woman called by her initials."

"She isn't called by her initials. That is her name—D-E-E C-E-E," Martha spelled it out.

"But her short hair and men's clothes?"

"We wear boys clothes because they are better for riding and outside work," Martha explained.

Dee Cee said, "And more comfortable and warmer."

"But mainly because around here, it is safer to be a man," Ruby added.

Schell once again held out his hand to Dee Cee. "You certainly fooled me. In all our confrontations, you have bested both me and Walker—that is before tonight."

Dee Cee winced.

"I've admired you as an adversary," Schell continued. He couldn't explain why he suddenly felt betrayed. Or, embarrassed? But since everyone else was in such a good mood, and Walking Owl seemed not the least put out that he—she—was a woman, he said politely, "I'd be honored to call you my friend."

Dee Cee did not take his extended hand. With her former serious expression, she studied his face, his black hair reaching his shoulders, his deep blue eyes under thick eyebrows, and beard and mustache almost hiding his full lips. "I still ain't positive sure you're Schell."

"Okay, fair enough. I guess I have changed a lot from the kid I was when I left here. So have you from that skinny freckle-faced girl with long red pigtails. So, ask me something that only Schell Campbell would know."

Dee Cee's forehead wrinkled in thought. Schell studied her thin face which lighted up with her beautiful smile when she decided what to ask. "When I beat you in that foot race at the Deerfield picnic, what did I do afterwards?"

Schell laughed. The constraint and wariness he'd maintained all evening completely disappeared. His eyes twinkled as he said, "You stuck out your tongue at me and said, 'That'll show you that a river rat can whup a prairie chicken anytime.'"

Again the room exploded with laughter, this time laughing at Dee Cee.

Blushing again, she tossed her head arrogantly, the short auburn waves bouncing on her forehead. "And we still can."

"Yes, Dee Cee, you've proved that. Now do you believe me?"

She nodded. Martha clapped her hands. The brothers whooped their pleasure. Ruby's happy smile effaced the age lines around her eyes.

Before returning to The Hump; the group decided that Martha should remain with the McFalls until Schell's house was finished, and maybe until after Cynthia arrived. Joining forces, the two groups made plans for mutual protection from bushwhackers. Ruby taught the men the bird call signals. Walking Owl promised to teach them how to send smoke signals, since the whistle calls wouldn't carry between their houses. Dee Cee warned them to watch the herd closely for rustlers.

Schell was pleased; his mission was a complete success. Instead of a troublesome enemy, he'd found the survivor of his family and made valuable friends of his nearest neighbors—Ruby and the boys. But whenever he thought of that tomboy, Dee Cee, the unpleasant sensation returned. Small matter.

His next job was to get everything ready for Cynthia. Assured by Ruby that the title to his land was clear, that the official Vernon County papers escaped the burning, having been secured in Ft. Scott until the war ended, Schell did not go to Nevada City, but to the closer village of Deerfield to get the supplies he needed to finish his house.

Leaving Walking Owl at The Hump, he rode to Deerfield. Ruby insisted that Dee Cee accompany him. There he purchased a good used wagon to haul home the windows, hardware, and other building supplies he needed. He had to admit that Dee Cee came in handy, not only by introducing him to the merchants, but with advice on buying household items Cynthia would need—cooking and eating utensils, a cook stove, buckets, and other household necessities. Schell made two more trips alone to haul his purchases home.

Since the general store at Deerfield didn't have furniture, again with Dee Cee accompanying him on her pony, he drove the mules and wagon twenty miles across the state line to Ft. Scott, returning the next day. Not only did he purchase the necessary items—tables, chairs, a dresser, and a bed, but on Dee Cee's suggestion, some fabric for curtains.

Coming home from Ft. Scott, after they left the road to cut across the prairie to The Hump, Dee Cee walked her pony beside the loaded wagon. The day was beautiful— the comfortably warm breeze of late May fanned against their cheeks.

"It's jest perfect," she said almost to herself, spreading out her left arm to encompass the landscape before them. "It's like ever'thing is welcomin' us home."

Sitting up in the wagon seat Schell was thinking the

same thing. He never tired of looking over the lush grasses, especially when The Hump filled in the background. To-day the prairie was sprinkled with daisies; their white heads seemed to be nodding assent in the intermittent breezes.

"Yes," Schell breathed, appreciating the beauty. Then he sighed. "Such potential. And so calm now it's hard to envision this as the scene of all that bloodshed in both our families."

Dee Cee nodded her head. "Do you think our folks were right to stick it out here?"

"Yeah," Schell answered sadly. "What about you? You wanting to stay?"

Dee Cee looked again at the view which now showed the border of trees which protected her home. "Yes. The land is good. We can't give in to scum and outlaws."

"No, we can't."

They rode on for a few minutes thinking of their dead family members.

"There's a good future here fer you and my brothers," Dee Cee said. "With our land, after things settle down more, the boys should do well. Trappin' is 'bout done fer. Cattle and farmin', that's the future fer them."

"And your future?" Schell looked at her, studying her attractive face, the determined tilt of her head, and her strong, lithe body at one with her horse.

"My future is here, too." She indicated her male clothing and her man's saddle and laughed. Her face crinkled up into a cute mischievous grim. "Can you see me at an af-ternoon tea in New York?"

Schell shook his head and joined her in laughing at the incongruous picture of her in a long silk dress pouring tea and carrying on chit-chat with Cynthia's fashionable friends.

They reached the trail into the timber to her house. Still in her impish mood, with a pasted, artificial smile, she held out her hand as if to have him kiss it, but instead withdrew it quickly with a mocking face. She spurred her pinto to a canter, and just before disappearing into the woods, turned back to Schell, grinned merrily and waved.

Schell drove his team and wagon the short distance to The Hump feeling happier than he had since discovering Martha still alive. He whistled "Soldier's Joy," as his weary mules plodded up the twisting lane to the summit.

Dee Cee and Martha came to The Hump almost every day, helping in many ways. Dee Cee was as adept in the house as she was on horseback, trapping, and tending to the stock. Though the McFalls relied mainly on their trapping for their living, they also ran some cattle on the free range west of the river. Schell soon became accustomed to Dee Cee's boyish appearance and manly skills. In spite of his waning resentment of her, he realized that she was his most helpful and capable neighbor.

With the additional help from the McFall brothers, and Ruby and Martha sewing for him, the house was soon built and furnished. Though not the fine house he left six years ago, the one room with a lean-to kitchen on the back was comfortable and homey.

In the warm June sunshine, Schell surveyed it with satisfaction. At last, after the years of war, he would begin his life with his bride. Perhaps the house wasn't what Cynthia expected, but she'd understand. They could manage with it until fall when he sold his young calves and had money to build more rooms. The funds his father left must be saved for herd expansion, equipment, barns, and other ranching needs.

Resting on his favorite perch on the lookout rock, he smiled as he listened to Martha sing as she hung the last curtain in the little gable window. She had fixed a cozy nook for herself in the loft above the one big room. Martha smoothed out the quilt Ruby gave her over the pallet she had fixed on the floor, and climbed down the ladder to the room below to spread the homemade sheets on the big bed. Though it was supposed to be a secret, Schell knew that the bright comforter she and Ruby were working on each evening for his wedding present would soon be ready to spread on his bed. His and Cynthia's! He hugged that thought to himself.

Even though Martha had fixed up her room, she did not move in. Shy about meeting Cynthia, she decided she should wait until Schell and his bride had settled in before joining them.

From the lookout rock, Schell also surveyed his land. About half a mile south of the foot of The Hump, Walking Owl, with Harris's help in keeping the herd in a tight group, was inspecting one of the newest calves. He signaled Schell that it was a bull calf and doing well. This calf was the last. All the cows had safely calved and most were bred again. The herd was thriving on the grass that was now waist high in areas where they had not grazed. Schell had difficulty spotting some of the calves in the waving grass. He was pleased.

He watched two riders nearing The Hump from the north. He recognized Dee Cee and Buddy with bags of flour and cornmeal strapped behind the saddles across the ponies' rumps. They had volunteered to bring Schell some meal the next time they took their pelts to trade.

Schell smiled again as he watched Dee Cee glide effortlessly on her pony. The pair circled The Hump to the trail, and slowing their ponies to a walk, climbed to the top. Schell rose to greet them, calling to Martha to let her know they were back. Anticipating the red and white striped stick candy Schell always ordered for her, Martha ran out laughing.

*What a difference in her*, Schell thought. No longer pale and sad, Martha bounced around the ponies until Dee Cee handed her the little sack of candy.

Buddy and Schell unloaded his supplies. Expecting their return, Martha had some coffee ready. The McFalls, Schell, and Martha relaxed around the new table with its bright checkered cloth, sipping the strong, black drink from new mugs.

"Oh, I 'most forgot," Dee Cee said, pulling a letter from her shirt pocket. "Here's a letter for you from *New York*."

Everyone laughed when Schell grabbed it and read the return address. "How'd you know it was from New York? I thought you couldn't read."

"Who said I couldn't? I can read. Ma can't."

Schell tore open the envelope. As he read its contents, his smile faded into a puzzled frown. Then he stood up.

"She's on her way already," he said excited, yet worried. "She said she couldn't wait to hear from me, but after she got the letter I sent from Independence, she decided to come on earlier than planned. She wrote here, 'Won't it be fun if I surprise you by arriving before this letter?' "

Schell was too excited and flustered to read more. "But we're not ready for her yet," he said disappointedly.

"When's she comin'?" Dee Cee asked.

Schell read the letter. "She said she was leaving the next day."

"What's the date on the letter?"

"May 20."

"Oh! How long does it take to git here?"

"A week on the train to Independence, and four or five days from Independence on the stage to Nevada City."

The four sitting at the table looked at one another in dismay. It was June 4—the letter was written fifteen days ago, plenty of time for her to get here.

"What'll I do?" Schell pulled on his beard, his forehead wrinkled in worry. "She wasn't supposed to come for another month. I was going to meet her in Independence and bring her down here."

Dee Cee shaded her eyes looking out the open door as if expecting to see Cynthia standing on the threshold. "We better get ready."

They all stood up eager to do something, but not knowing what. Dee Cee, as usual, knew what to do. "Buddy, get on home and tell Ma about the letter. Tell her to bake up some extra bread and food for Schell's bride. I'll be home soon."

While Schell finished reading the letter, smiling to himself at the message at the end, Dee Cee and Martha were scurrying around putting the house in order. Engrossed with his letter, Schell did not at first notice the bobwhite call (which meant rider approaching) that was repeated two times (two riders), followed by a pause and then two more calls. At the first signal, Martha gasped, putting her hands over her mouth to keep from crying out. Dee Cee gave Martha a reassuring pat as she ran out the door toward her pony for her rifle. Then she was at the lookout rock to see who the two riders were.

Alerted by Dee Cee's and Martha's alarm, and understanding the meaning of Walking Owl's bird calls, Schell hurried to the rock, arriving there just when the Osage jumped off his horse, followed closely by the panting dog. About a mile away, approaching slowly from the northeast, the direction from Nevada City, were two riders—a brightly dressed woman with a red parasol, followed by a man and a pack mule loaded with baggage.

"Cynthia?" Dee Cee asked in relief.

"Yes. Cynthia. Oh my . . ." Still holding the letter in his hand, he turned to Walking Owl, showing the letter. "She's coming now," he explained. "What'll I do?"

"Take my horse and go meet her, I'd say," Walking Owl said.

Schell jammed the letter into his pocket, mounted the bay and started down the trail.

"He's in a daze," Dee Cee laughed.

Walking Owl grunted agreement. Suddenly his eyes squinted as, almost out of his vision, he saw something rapidly approaching down the straight, section line road. He gave three piercing bobwhite calls to alert Schell, paused, and repeated. Dee Cee also saw the horsemen fast approaching the unsuspecting man and woman. She jumped on her pinto just as Schell reappeared.

"Marthie," she said calmly. "Git in one of them pits." She motioned to Schell that she was planning to circle around to come in behind the riders and then galloped over the western ridge.

Martha stood there, shocked into inactivity, looking at Schell.

"Better do as she said," he said gently, patting her shoulder. "We'll take care of those men."

"Better yet, Martha, you can help. Come with me," Walking Owl said. He ran to the house for an ember from the stove which he put into a pan. "Can you make the smoke signals we learned?"

She nodded her head.

"Good. This time you won't have to hide. You can help. Take Harris with you and ride your pony to the southern slope out of sight of the riders and signal the McFalls. Then stay south of The Hump and get back to the river."

The child nodded again, grabbed her pony that was tethered to a tree, and taking the gun Schell handed her, rode out of their sight, Harris by her side.

Schell had saddled Solomon and gathered up ammunition for both men.

They glanced quickly at the plodding pair who were still unaware of their pursuers. Speaking rapidly as they mounted, the men made their plans. "Cynthia and her guide won't make it to the trail up here before those bushwhackers get to them." Schell said, "So I'll ride out on the road to Cynthia and try to get them back here. You circle round from the east. Dee Cee will come in from the west." Schell pointed down on the prairie to Dee Cee who, half hidden in the tall grass, was doing just that.

Already on his way, Walking Owl called back, "With any luck I should reach them about the time Dee Cee does."

Schell loped his horse behind Walking Owl down the trail. When his friend disappeared east over the slight rise in the prairie to come in on the men from their left, Schell galloped down the road in plain view. Cynthia and her guide were only about a half mile away. Whistling, waving his hat in the air, and calling her name, he hoped to alert the pair to the danger behind them, yet not scare them into running from him.

He could no longer see Dee Cee's or Walking Owl's movements, but he did look back to the skyline over The Hump to see Martha's smoke signals to the McFalls. Dear Martha. He prayed that this day would not leave her with more sorrow.

"Cynthia! Cynthia!" he called. "Hurry!"

The guide behind Cynthia pulled up sharp. He then looked behind him and noticed for the first time the three pursuers. With a yell, he dropped the rope to the pack mule, kicked his horse savagely in its sides, and veered off to the east across the grass as fast as his mount would go. The mule trotted off in the opposite direction.

Surprised, Cynthia, not understanding what was happening, nor realizing there was any danger to herself, trotted after the mule that carried her trousseau and all the belongings she brought to start housekeeping. Though recognizing Schell right away, she mistook his mad rush for joy at seeing her after being parted for almost three months. Greeting him could wait. Catching the pack mule could not.

Appalled, Schell watched her turn off the road and increase her speed after the runaway mule. Schell started to cut across the prairie to her when gunshots struck close to him. One of the riders was rapidly approaching down the road. The other two were plowing through the tall grass toward Cynthia.

"Let the baggage go," Schell shouted, hoping she could

hear him for they were less than a quarter of a mile apart. "That's what they want."

Cynthia looked back amazed. Not until she heard the shots directed at Schell and realized that the men were chasing her was she aware of her danger.

"Run," Schell shouted, galloping still closer to her. "Get to the woods."

In horror Cynthia saw the two men thrashing through the grass toward her and the other one after Schell. There was a single shot—Schell aiming at the man chasing him, and then a volley of shots at Schell and at Cynthia. When the first shot struck the ground near her horse, he reared, causing Cynthia to drop her reins. Grasping the horse's mane, she retained her seat on the sidesaddle. Her horse bolted away from the chasing men.

Unable to catch her, but keeping ahead of the attackers, Schell raced after Cynthia. He was aware that he was out-distancing his one pursuer. Hearing shots from behind that man, he knew that Walking Owl was on the scene. To stop those chasing Cynthia, he galloped Solomon across their line of fire between them and Cynthia to divert them. At the same time he again heard the welcome sound of Walking Owl's rifle which was now behind these two men.

Distracted by Schell and Walking Owl, the bushwhackers did not see Dee Cee cutting across the prairie toward Cynthia's runaway mount because she had been hidden by the tall grass and by the swell in the ground. Reaching Cynthia, Dee Cee rode beside her for a few rods, slowing down Cynthia's horse by forcing it to run in tight circles.

To evade Schell, one of the outlaws swung his powerful and swift horse to the south. Seeing both girls, the outlaw lifted his pistol to aim. With their horses neck and neck,

Dee Cee pulled Cynthia off just as a bullet skimmed Cynthia's saddle. The girls rolled unhurt onto the soft, wet ground; their horses galloped frantically across to the timber along the river.

Thinking he shot one of the girls, the gunman headed his big sorrel stallion to the spot where they fell, but Schell's fire forced him to change his direction.

Cynthia, mistaking Dee Cee for one of the outlaws, struggled out of her grasp, but her long riding shirt wrapped around her legs and prevented her from getting up. She started to scream. Dee Cee clamped her hand over her mouth and hissed, "Keep down. I'm Schell's friend. And for heavens sake, don't yell."

To make sure, Dee Cee forcibly held her down while she parted the grass above them to see where the bushwhacker was. "Follow me," she whispered. "No, don't get up, crawl."

Dee Cee crawled swiftly through the thick grass. At first she had to almost pull the terrified girl, but Cynthia soon caught on that her rude companion was trying to hide them in the grass to elude the attackers. Cynthia crawled after her readily, though greatly hampered by her bulky skirts and shortness of breath because of her tight corset.

Green and supple, the grass sprung back after they passed, leaving no trail. As the horseman drew near, Dee Cee shoved Cynthia down on her stomach, unintentionally mashing her face in the ground. Dee Cee lay prone beside her with her finger to her lips warning Cynthia to be quiet. Cynthia gasped from her mouthful of mud. To assure she keep quiet, once again Dee Cee clamped her hand over Cynthia's mouth, shaking her head vigorously, her eyes frightening in their intensity.

Not finding the girls and pressed by Schell's fire, the bushwhacker shot at Schell while heading for the nearest cover; the timber into which the two horses and mule just vanished.

The last shot grazed Schell. He grabbed his arm; though bleeding, it was not serious. Seeing about his wound and uncertain about whether to go to Cynthia or catch the outlaw, Schell hesitated enough for the bushwhacker to reach the edge of the timber.

A new volley of shots came from the trees. The rider jerked, grabbed his leg, pulled back roughly on his reins, turned, and fled north on his powerful horse. The McFall brothers and Ruby stepped out from behind the trees just as Walking Owl loped up behind Schell.

The Osage nodded to answer his friend's unspoken question. "All clear. All three ran off," he said. "We winged two of them."

Schell's long-awaited reunion with Cynthia did not go as he had anticipated. When Dee Cee attempted to help her stand up, she shook her off with distaste. With difficulty, because the heel of a boot was tangled in her skirts, Cynthia stood up to see Schell jump off Solomon beside her. She was distraught and humiliated—her dress muddy, torn, and grass-stained. Her hat was gone and her long, blond hair, loosened from the bun in the back, was full of seeds and dried stalks. Tears streaked down her face, mud-caked and scratched from the sharp grass blades. Angry sparks flew from her tear-brimmed eyes as she sputtered incoherent words.

Schell tried to comfort her. "Cynthia, my poor darling, I'm so sorry." He could think of nothing to say except to apologize over and over. He took Cynthia in his arms and held her tight, kissing her. She hung on to him, burying her head in his shoulder, breathing hard from her exertion and emotions. "There, there, my darling. You're safe now. It's all over."

When she stopped trembling, she looked up. In a circle around her, in addition to Dee Cee, whom she recognized as the youth who knocked her off her horse, were the worried faces of Walking Owl, Ruby, Buddy, Red, and Martha. Even Harris, his tongue hanging out from his running, was silently staring at her, his brown eyes sad.

Before she could react to these people who had seemingly sprung from the ground, Schell said, "These, my darling, are my family and my good neighbors, the McFalls." Over her head he thanked each one with his eyes. "Everyone of these people in one way or another saved you from the bushwhackers."

Cynthia tried to smile, to be polite, but was still too distressed. She only nodded. When she could talk, the first thing she asked was, "My baggage?"

"Here it is," Buddy said. She hadn't noticed that he held the lead rope of the mule with its load unharmed or that Red held her horse.

Everyone returned to The Hump, where Schell briefly told Cynthia about the bushwhackers, his family tragedy, and the burned-out buildings. While the McFall brothers were seeing to the horses, Dee Cee and Walking Owl were bringing in Cynthia's baggage. Ruby and Martha prepared a snack.

Cynthia was pleasant to everyone but Dee Cee. Whenever Dee Cee came near her, Cynthia shuddered, unconsciously drawing away. When Dee Cee made her last trip out for the bags, Cynthia whispered to Schell. "Why do you allow that repulsive boy in the house?"

"What boy?" Schell asked surprised. By now he was so used to Dee Cee that he forgot that strangers mistook her for a boy, as he himself did at first.

"That one out there. That D. C. He's as bad as one of the outlaws."

"Oh! Dee Cee?" Schell grinned. "*She's* not a boy. She's a woman about your age."

Cynthia stared at Dee Cee, who entered the room carrying a heavy bag easily. "A woman!" She surveyed Dee Cee's slim figure, boyish haircut, her muddy trousers, and oversized man's shirt. "What kind of women do you have out here?"

Shocked at Cynthia's ingratitude and insensitivity, yet realizing how inadequately prepared she was for all she'd been through today, Schell answered softly, "The kind that is willing to risk being shot to save your life. If she hadn't pulled you off your horse, you would be lying face down on the prairie with a bullet in your back."

## Chapter Five

Cynthia stared at Dee Cee open-mouthed. She then looked at Schell who was smiling his gratitude and thanks at Dee Cee.

"She didn't know, Schell," Dee Cee said. "She probably thinks I'm as bad as one of the bushwhackers." Turning to Cynthia she said, "Sorry I was so rough. Didn't have time to explain, but that feller chasin' you had his sights on you. All I could think to do was to knock you off your horse out of his line of fire."

"I've ruined everything," Cynthia said to Schell.

"No, you haven't," Schell said gently.

"I thought I was going to give you such a nice surprise—show you how capable I was to live in the West by coming out here by myself."

"You got within sight of Campbell's Hump all by yourself. You almost made it," Schell said, putting his right arm around her again.

"Everything was going so well—the train trip and all. It was so romantic riding to you across the mountains and through all that beautiful farm land in Illinois and Indiana.

I envisioned your house like those big houses I saw. Even when I got to Independence everything went well. I stayed in a nice inn, and all by myself got the stage. Just like the books I've read—the grizzly driver and a man sitting beside him with a gun. Oh, it was thrilling."

"Did the ride go well?"

"Well, it didn't take me long to learn that it wasn't romantic at all. The dust was awful. The roads were so poor that I jolted all the time. I'm black and blue from bouncing so much. And the rest facilities!" Her whole body shuddered in revulsion.

"But I survived them, and yesterday morning right on time we arrived in Nevada City. That's sure the wrong name. A city! Just some dreary little shacks. There's no city there, no inn, no livery stable to rent a horse, or anything."

"The Union Army burned it down," Ruby explained. "They're just now rebuilding it."

Cynthia curled up her lip in distaste, conveying that the country must have deserved what it got.

"But you did get a horse," Martha said.

"Yes, I haven't gotten to that." She smiled at the child, patting her arm. She continued her story talking to Schell. "See, I planned on coming out here yesterday since I remembered you telling me it was only ten miles. I could easily make that on horseback."

She spoke to Dee Cee, "I'm a good rider. I don't fall off unless knocked off." She then turned back to Schell, "But I couldn't rent any horses or get anyone to guide me. I spent all yesterday trying to hire someone. Nobody would come. I ended up having to buy my horse and the pack mule after I finally persuaded one surly fellow to show me the way. I had to pay him twice what he should have got. And I paid a high price to a young couple for putting me up last night in just a hovel of a house." She again shuddered remembering her ordeal.

She brushed some dried mud off her skirt. "Things sure are expensive out here."

"Yes, everything costs more in the West. And as you found out, it's lots different out here from New York. Not many roads, no bridges, not many railroads. Then there is the constant danger of outlaws, so freight costs are sky-high," Schell explained.

"People in town knowed you was headed out here to Campbell's Hump?" Ruby asked.

"Sure, practically everyone in town. What's wrong with that?"

"We don't never tell strangers where we're goin'," Ruby said.

"We don't unless we're hankerin' to be shot," Dee Cee added.

"Oh. I didn't know."

"Of course, you didn't," Schell said sliding his hand over her cheek. He winced when he moved his injured left arm.

"But those hicks in town did know about this place, I could tell; they either acted like they'd never heard of it, or told me straight out that they wouldn't take me. Was it because of outlaws like those men that chased me that I couldn't hire anyone?"

"Yes," Ruby said. "We never travel the main roads or let anyone know when or where we're going."

"And you live like this *all the time*?" Cynthia asked appalled.

"We trust it will get better. When more people like Schell here move in, we'll run the bushwhackers out of the country."

Schell said, "But you did persuade that one fellow to guide you."

"Lot of good he did, running off like that. All the time; after we got a couple of miles out of town, he kept looking back. I didn't understand why he did that. I guess he was expecting something?"

"Any fool would expect trouble. I'm surprised you got him to come at all," Dee Cee said.

"Well, he was in a big hurry, tried to make me canter most of the way. I wouldn't because I wanted to look my best when I first saw you, Schell. I didn't want to get all hot and sweaty." She looked at her torn skirt, scratched hands, and muddy boots that still showed the effect of her ordeal even though she and Martha had done some cosmetic repairs when she first reached the house.

Then, completely changing her mood, she recognized the irony in what she just said. The corners of her mouth turned up into a cute, endearing smile. "I wanted to arrive the elegant lady from New York." She pursed her lips in an exaggerated manner, held her head in a haughty position, and lifted her coffee mug with thumb and forefinger, her little finger extended.

Everyone laughed, Cynthia most of all. Then she became serious. "I guess those men followed me out of town to . . . What do you call it?"

"Bushwhack you," Dee Cee said.

"Yes, bushwhack me. What a word, but descriptive. And I set myself up for it?"

"I'm afraid so," Ruby said.

"What would they have done if you all hadn't rescued me?"

"Taken your baggage and horses and shot you after they . . ." Dee Cee paused, "You know what they would have done."

"Oh!" Cynthia's face showed more horror and fear than when she was actually in danger. "I thought the code of the west was to protect women?"

"It is," Schell said gently. "Believe me it still is, but those brutes are not western men, but the worst of society taking advantage of the war and its aftermath to do as they wish. There is no law here to stop them."

"Not yet," Ruby said. "But we're gonna remedy that."

Everyone's attention had been so concentrated on Cynthia that no one had noticed that Schell's face was ashy, or that he wobbled just a bit. The small amount of bleeding from his wound had dried.

Dee Cee noticed his lips held tight and the pain in his eyes. "Schell's been hit" she exclaimed in alarm, going to him.

"Just grazed," he said as if it was of no importance. His knees gave out and he would have fallen had Walking Owl not caught him.

"Oh, my brave darling," Cynthia cried, rushing to him.

"I guess I'm still not back to normal from my war wounds," Schell apologized lying on the bed where Walking Owl laid him.

Instantly Cynthia became a different person. From the crying, clinging victim, she became a competent nurse. She removed Schell's shirt, ordered hot water and clean cloths. "The wound is just on the surface. He's more in shock than anything. Keep him covered. Get him some hot coffee." There before his eyes was the woman Schell had fallen in love with. He let her minister to him.

Schell's dizzy spell was over in a few minutes. His wound ceased to throb. He insisted on sitting up, saying that he was all right now. Cynthia sat beside him, holding his hands.

Ruby always speaking what was on her mind, asked, "When are you two gettin' hitched?"

Taken back, Schell stammered, glancing at Cynthia, "I don't know. She got here so unexpected."

"I hear the circuit ridin' preacher will be comin' to Deerfield soon. You could ride over there and he'd tie the knot quick enough in between his preachin'. May not be another chance for weeks," Ruby said.

Cynthia's lips turned down at the corners. She shot an agonized appeal to Schell. "No wedding?" She ran to one of the bags Dee Cee had placed by the bed and pulled out a white satin dress. "See, I've got all my wedding clothes here, veil, train and everything. I planned on a big church wedding."

The McFalls laughed, Buddy and Red loudest of all. Dee Cee tapped Buddy quickly to silence him. Though she was also grinning, she composed her face and explained patiently to Cynthia, "There's no churches still a-standin' in this county. Not even a justice of the peace. There ain't been no legal marriages since the war started. Even now the only ones who can marry people are the circuit riders who sometimes come through. This one at Deerfield will be the first one in years."

"They ain't wantin' to git shot," Ruby explained. "Preachers is fair game for the bushwhackers."

Cynthia looked from them to Schell and back, panic on her face.

Ruby and Dee Cee stood up at the same time. "I reckon we best leave you two to work things out," Ruby said, motioning to her sons to get going. Looking from Schell to Cynthia, she added, "Want one of us to stay the night?"

After the outlaw attack, the bloodshed, and the narrowly thwarted assault on Cynthia, Schell was amused at Ruby's thinking of the improprieties of a man and woman being alone for a night when not married. *I guess civilization will survive here, after all*, he thought.

"Yes," Cynthia replied quickly, surprising Schell. He thought she would be the last person to want anyone else with them. "Yes, that would be very kind of you. Could Martha stay the night?"

Cynthia looked at the coverless bed and Martha's feeble attempts to pretty up the stark room. Although the cracks in the walls were plastered over, those in the split-log floor were not. In places the ground below was visible. Spiders, snakes, and no telling what else could freely enter.

She quivered in distaste. "Please, everyone else leave, you too, Schell, while Martha and I see to my clothes." Expecting immediate obedience, she opened another bag and pulled out a thin navy dress with a white lace collar.

Buddy snickered again, before Dee Cee cuffed him. Ruby shooed everyone out, but not before they heard Cynthia mutter, "An ignoramus, two boorish hicks, a savage Indian, and that insufferable . . ." she paused to find the word to describe Dee Cee, "that she-bear." She then turned to Martha, giving her orders about her clothes and fixing a meal.

Pushed out of his house, Schell, still a bit light-headed

from his near fainting, sat on the front stoop in a swirl of emotions. Ruby patted his shoulder as she passed by him toward her mare tied by the house.

Just before she mounted she asked Dee Cee, "Did you recognize the bushwhackers?"

"Yes. Hank Teller."

Ruby gritted her teeth. "Did the boys recognize him?"

"I don't know. They were pretty far away."

Ruby put her foot into her stirrup and swung easily into the saddle, arranging her skirt in the seat as she sat astride. "Keep a close watch, Schell. That devil will be back. He won't forget us clipping him like that." She followed her children into the setting sun toward The Hump's ridge, where their recent comings and goings from the river had made a path.

Schell nodded his understanding. Almost numb from the emotions of the day's events, this last news bounced off scarcely heeded. No urgency there; the man was wounded. But Cynthia! Inside, he heard her scurrying around, talking to Martha, and generally taking over. That was what he wanted, what he needed. A partner in his house as well as in his heart and for all his life. His Cynthia was here, right now, ready to fill that role, nothing hurt except her pride.

He must overlook her behavior this afternoon. *After a good night's sleep, she'll see things differently*. But nagging at him from the back of his mind was the troubling thought that no matter how distraught she was from her close brush with death, she should not have treated his friends the way she did.

Walking Owl was at the lookout rock scanning the country, turning from the scene of the recent scrimmage in the north to the south where the cattle were resting and chewing their cuds. He unconsciously patted Harris on the head, and then walked over to the temporary camp where he and Schell still lived. Schell joined him, sitting on the makeshift chair he had hammered together from boards retrieved from the ashes. For once Schell was the silent one.

"She's got lots of spunk," Walking Owl said.

"Yes, she has."

Walking Owl was frying their supper over a fire. "Pretty, too." Knowing his friend's need to talk things out, Walking Owl tried to encourage him.

"Very."

A lone coyote howled in the dusky light, followed by the yip-yipping of many more.

Walking Owl tried again. "She went through a lot today. Most women brought up like her would have fainted or become hysterical."

"I know."

"Then forget those things she said."

"How can I? Calling you a savage? You are more educated and gentle than any man I know."

"She knows only what she's heard."

"And Dee Cee? How can she say that?"

"She didn't mean it. She was upset."

The men ate their meal quickly as always, throwing Harris the scraps.

"I think I'll just go tell her and Martha goodnight," Schell said. Walking Owl grunted his approval.

When Schell returned an hour later and crawled into his bedroll, Walking Owl raised up on one elbow.

"Good night, Walker." Though no longer bitter, Schell's voice was sad. Guessing Walking Owl's thoughts, he added, "I've not forgotten my part of our bargain to accompany you to Blue Mounds. Cynthia's coming before we got a chance to go will not make any difference."

"I never doubted you." Walking Owl turned over and was soon sleeping the quiet, snoreless sleep of the Osages.

Schell didn't sleep much that night.

Harris's joyful greeting to Martha awakened Schell. Not realizing he had finally fallen asleep, he was surprised to see the sun already clear of the horizon and Walking Owl's empty bed.

"Hey, early bird," he started to tease Martha, but seeing her sober face, he asked, "What's the matter?"

"You better come to the house," she said, pulling him up.

When they entered the house, he saw that Cynthia had everything packed and was waiting in her riding clothes.

"What're you doing?" Schell stammered.

"Leaving. I won't stay another day in this forsaken place. I didn't sleep all night for fear of snakes, and those awful animals."

Schell looked to Martha for explanation.

"Coyotes. They scared her."

"Those hellish coyotes," Cynthia continued, her voice rising with each word. "And the people around here, those stupid men in town. Getting shot at, being married by a man on horseback, no decent place to live!" She was trembling. "I won't stay."

Schell put his arms around her. "It will be all right. This trouble is just a temporary condition. This is good land, beautiful land to spend our lives on. Just look at that view." He pulled her to the door where she could see the mist hanging in the draws and the dew shining on the miles of grass now motionless in the early morning calm. In spite of Cynthia's announcement, he felt renewed by the superb scene.

"I hate it," Cynthia cried. "Boring, endless nothingness. Nothing but sharp blades, briars, with outlaws and probably Indians lurking in every one of those low places to waylay innocent women. I'd die if I had to live here."

"There, there, my darling, you just had a bad time. You'll grow to love it as I do."

Cynthia broke away from his arms. "Never. And Schell, you don't belong here, either. Take me back to New York. That job in Daddy's firm is still open for you. We can catch the afternoon stage in Nevada City and be back there in no time. I've got it all worked out. We can have that wedding in Independence. *They* have churches there. I saw a pretty one near the train station. Then for a honeymoon . . ."

Schell put his hand over her mouth, "No, Cynthia, I can't. I have obligations here."

"I thought you'd say that. All right then, I'll go on ahead and get things ready. We can be married in our church. You take care of what you have to do here and come later."

Schell looked at Martha, who had tears in her eyes. Would she be happy in the East? And Walking Owl? A combination brother, father, partner, and best friend. No, he couldn't leave him after all the Osage had done for him in the past few weeks. Getting by this far would have been impossible without him. Schell also knew that in a different way, Walking Owl needed him as much as Martha did. He was convinced that both of their futures were at Campbell's Hump.

And the McFalls? Well, he didn't need to worry about them. They sure could take care of themselves, but in the past weeks he had learned to admire them, treating the boys as brothers and Ruby as a substitute mother.

Dee Cee? Sister, brother, friend. She was all those, for she had qualities that were admirable in both sexes.

No, he couldn't leave.

Cynthia's ultimatum rang in his ears, "Schell, I'm leaving. Are you going to come?"

He looked at this delectable woman—the subject of his waking and sleeping dreams for the year he had known her, the reason for all his labor and plans for the ranch. As he studied her beautiful face and proud carriage, he knew that if he did not go with her, his happy plans for their future together would crumble around him. He would be alone and empty out on this vacant prairie. To have her he had been willing to fight the whole world. And she was his.

He opened his mouth to agree, but instead said sadly, tears streaming down his face, "No, Cynthia, I can't come with you. My place is here."

Dumbfounded by his answer, Cynthia began to cry, frustrated by his refusal. Her dream was also over. She had lost him.

Walking Owl picked up several of her bags. "I'll saddle your gelding and load these on your mule. I'll see you safely to the stage."

Cynthia nodded agreement. While Martha and Walking Owl got the horses ready and loaded, Cynthia gave Schell a farewell hug. "I'm sorry, Schell. Neither of us is the same person out here that we were back home. Don't you see how miserable both of us would be if I stayed here?

It just wouldn't do. I'll always remember you with bullets flying around you as you galloped across the prairie to save me. You were magnificent."

Schell could not speak because of the lump in his throat. Her long hair stylishly arranged on her head, her trim body correctly clothed in the latest fashion of riding garments, she was the lady he had fallen in love with. Even with the prairie breeze blowing a wisp of hair against her face, she was again the woman he admired during his long convalescence when she was one of the volunteer nurses in the veterans hospital.

Cynthia was right. This wild, raw country, though grand and exciting to him, was not the place for her.

"And I'll remember you as you are just this moment," Schell said, "beautiful, poised, and in control. Wise enough to know the best thing to do, and brave enough to carry it out. *You* are magnificent. Now go with Walker."

Standing hand in hand on the lookout rock beside the five graves of their family, Schell and Martha watched the pair wind down the trail and cut across the grass to the section line road that disappeared north into the morning haze. They did not move until the dots that were two mounted riders and a loaded mule faded into the distance.

"Little sister," Schell said. "we should go to the McFalls for your things. You are now the lady of the house on Campbell's Hump. I hope you won't mind keeping house for two old bachelors."

Martha hugged Schell, the brightness back in her face. "I'll take care of you forever and ever."

"Well, perhaps not that long." Schell laughed. "One of these days when you grow up, you'll find a fine young man."

## Chapter Six

Schell removed his army hat and rubbed the back of his right forearm over his forehead to wipe off the perspiration that was threatening his eyes. The southwest wind behind him ruffled his hair as it cooled the man.

"I'd almost forgotten how hot it gets here in July," he said when he halted Solomon beside Walking Owl. The Osage had stopped when he turned east after crossing a creek valley and emerging from the dense cover of trees that clung to the low area where the creek wound through the prairie. The bluestem grass had grown to its full height. In the richer loam nearer the creek, it almost reached the saddle horn. For protection against the sharp mature grass blades, the men had wrapped the horses' legs. To make the going easier for the horses, though it was farther, instead of cutting across the prairie, they traveled roads and trails.

The luminous green carpet of early spring had grown into a gray-green rolling sea as gusts of wind swept the grass into ripples of waves.

Walking Owl pointed northeast, his face a mixture of

emotions. "There it is, Schell. There's my childhood homeland."

About six or seven miles away, clearly visible in the clear, dry air, were several huge, treeless mounds. Like Campbell's Hump, each rising alone from the prairie, but in clusters as if for companionship.

"Blue Mounds?" Schell asked.

Walking Owl nodded. "We call them 'Crying Mounds' because it is a place for mourning and weeping. Pawhuska, my grandfather, is buried in a rock cairn on top the higher of those twin mounds there."

Tears streamed down Walking Owl's face as he turned to Schell. "I haven't been here for thirty-five years."

The horses swished their tails and stomped their feet against the flies attacking their sweaty bodies. Schell flexed his shoulders to ease his muscles after their long ride. The worst heat of the day was over, though behind them the sun was still high enough in the western sky to clear the wooded creek they just crossed.

"Tell me about your people, Walker. In these months since we've been together you've learned almost all there is to know about me, but I know very little about your past."

"Now that we are here it is the time to tell you," Walking Owl said. As the two men rode side by side down the section line wagon road that zigzagged east and north toward the mounds, Walking Owl told his story.

He was born in 1816 at Big Osage village on Old Town Creek, a tributary of the Marmaton River. Because the spring had dried up, the grass was overgrazed, and wood supplies exhausted with the increase in population, the people had already moved from the Blue Mounds area to a fresh area with plenty of water, grass, and wood. Walking Owl's mother's father was chief of the tribe. As a young warrior, before he became chief, Walking Owl's grandfather took part in the coalition of Indian tribes under the leadership of the Miami tribe. In 1791 on the Wabash River, they defeated the Americans. While "scalping" his opponent, his grandfather grabbed the soldier's white powdered wig. Bragging about his coup, he began wearing the wig, calling himself Pawhuska, or White Hair.

Pawhuska had traveled in the White world, to New Orleans, Washington, D. C., and other places, seeing the astonishing scope and power of the White world. He knew that in order to survive, the Osage had no choice but to cooperate with the Americans. Therefore, in 1808, in return for protection and friendship with the United States government, he ceded the Osage woodland areas in Arkansas and southern Missouri, except the thirty-mile strip along the Kansas border. He retained the borderland between the hilly woodland to the east and the western prairie, since that area was the location of their major villages. The Americans readily agreed that the Osages should retain that eastern portion of "the great American desert," for they believed that land was unsuitable for settlers.

Pawhuska knew that the Osage way of life had to change. Wanting his young people to learn the magic, or secret, of the White men's success, which he believed was inherent in their religion, Pawhuska asked for a mission school. In the year Missouri became a state, 1821, the United Foreign Missionary Society, mostly Presbyterians, set up a school, called Harmony Mission. The mission was located only a few miles from the Osage villages.

Walking Owl was sent to the mission school when he

was seven. There the other children and he lived as the Whites did. Willing and intelligent, he learned to speak English without an accent and read every book at the mission.

He returned to the tribe after three years, for the Osages moved to Kansas and then to Oklahoma, ceding the rest of their Missouri holdings. All of the mission children had a difficult time adjusting when they came home. Most of them died. Walking Owl was one of the few who survived the cultural shock though he never felt completely a part of the tribal way of life.

"So that's how come you can pass as a White man?" Schell asked.

"That and traveling, and my years in the army. Most of the time people don't know I'm not White. I even attended some university classes in Ohio for a time."

"Is that how you got your name?"

"Yes, my friends at the mission started it. When I wasn't reading I used to take long walks." While telling his story, Walking Owl's eyes darted from side to side studying the terrain as they traveled. "I suppose Harmony Mission succeeded somewhat with me, though it was a dismal failure for my people and the Americans. Their purpose was to teach us Christianity, farming, and to wean us away from our traditional life style of long seasonal hunts and trading furs and hides for the supplies we needed. But the missionary people never succeeded in changing us.

"I was different in one respect. I liked the learning fine. But Christianity? No. I let them preach all they wanted, but was not 'converted' as they wanted. I soon saw their belief was based on individuals acquiring material things, mainly land, rather than our belief of the tribe borrowing the land from the Great Force. Instead of striving for spiritual and physical harmony with the natural world, which is our way, I saw selfish exploitation in the name of a god who seemed to condone slaughtering the buffalo and plowing under the life-sustaining prairie grass."

Schell felt uncomfortable. His family had amassed a huge track of former Osage land, though the buffalo had already left before they arrived.

Walking Owl laughed at his guilty look. "It's already done, Schell. You didn't do it. One reason I was taken with you is that you love the land for what it is, not only what it will do for you. The land is here for us to use, to sustain our lives, but we should leave it as we found it for others to follow us, not change it to suit our temporary purposes."

As they approached the mounds, they passed several homesteads but saw no people. Probably everyone was inside out of the heat, Schell decided. So engrossed was Schell in their conversation that he failed to wonder why the two farmers they did meet on the road hurried past them and then stopped to stare at them.

The farther east they came, the larger the fields of cultivated ground and more signs of continued habitation from pre-war times. The tall houses and roomy barns were undamaged. These people, near the pro-Union Cedar County line and protected from the north by the unfordable Osage River, had not suffered as greatly from the armies and bushwhackers as Schell's area nearer the Kansas border.

"But you seem to have come around to the White way of thinking. You've talked about getting land." Schell said.

"Yes, I have. Pawhuska was wise enough to realize we had to change in order to survive. I agree. I've changed. Though I hate farming—ranching is okay. In this country, my owning some land is the only way I see now to live in unity with Wah-kon-tah."

"With what?"

"The Great Mystery Force."

"And the reason for this trip here?" Schell still didn't understand why his friend wanted to come, except for his natural desire to honor his grandfather's grave. He couldn't see why that duty was so urgent and what it had to do with Walker getting *his* land.

"Schell, you know who you are. Your American heritage has been uninterrupted, and you know where you belong. Even though you lost most of your family, you still have a sister and you still have the family land. You're having to fight for it, and it isn't going to be easy, but you know your way. You know it so well, that you let go of the woman you've been blabbing about ever since I first met you."

A frown creased Schell's forehead for just a second. "You understand it better than I do. You are right, Walker. I did break with Cynthia. You're saying that I did it because of my heritage. Because my place was here and hers wasn't?"

Walking Owl nodded. "Your family died preserving it for you."

"You see things so clearly. I've just been muddling along, not fully realizing what I was doing. I know that I made the right decision about Cynthia, though it still hurts like fury whenever I think of her." He unconsciously put his hand over his heart and took a deep breath.

Walking Owl was silent for a few minutes as their weary horses plodded on past a field of shoulder-high corn, its leaves curled to preserve moisture in the July heat.

"In your world," Walking Owl said, "living at this time in history is a beginning, a door opening to untold possibilities. For me in my world, living now is an end. It's as if the Great Mystery Force has blocked my path without giving me any clue where I can find the detour. Your family and land carry you on. My family is all dead. My land—this land—was lost in my childhood. Your heritage shows you the way. My heritage has died. I have no guide."

They had reached a small creek that still contained a trickle of water in spite of the dry summer. While they made camp for the night, Walking Owl continued. "I'm on the fringe of society, neither Osage nor White. Although I can live in either, I do not belong. The last time I was on the reservation, at my father's last illness and death before the war, I was a stranger to their new way of life. Nothing there for me."

Straightening up from hobbling the horses to let them graze, he put his hand on his hip and arched his back to relieve the tense muscles. "I'm also at a middle point in my life. I am neither young, nor old. If I'm ever going to find my place, if I ever achieve harmony, it must begin now." He spread out his blanket and lay down. "To do that I need to return here to the land that bore me, draw from it what it can give, and take back to Campbell's Hump what I find here, so that I can live with Wah-kon-tah the years left to me." When Walking Owl said no more, Schell knew he was asleep.

Schell's mind was too busy to drop instantly off to sleep

as his friend always did. Using his unneeded blanket for a pillow, he stared at the brightness of the stars. Around him was the usual night chorus: crickets, frogs, and the on-again-off-again serenade of the coyotes. He missed Harris curling up against him.

Harris, and Martha, and The Hump. The dark elevations he faced in the eastern sky reminded him of his mound. In spite of Ruby's assurance that everything would be all right at home, he worried.

After Cynthia's departure, he had thrown himself into rebuilding the ranch outbuildings. He and Walking Owl made several trips to town for lumber to build a barn, and because Walking Owl preferred not to live in the house, started a bunkhouse for him. Later when he reached the place where he could hire the crew he would eventually need to run his outfit, he would enlarge the building.

He had scoured the country to buy more cattle and horses, meeting the growing wave of settlers moving in, sharing their mutual need—mainly the need for law and order to protect them from the outlaws.

Added to his need to get the ranch running again, was the continual worry of Hank Teller's gang returning. He and Walking Owl always took turns with nightly watches.

Ruby promised that she and her children would look after Martha and the ranch. Since summer was a slack season for trapping, she offered to let Dee Cee stay on The Hump for the few days he and Walking Owl would be gone.

"I have to go with Walker, Ruby," Schell had explained early that morning before leaving. She and Dee Cee had ridden up before dawn. "It was part of our agreement. He's getting restless these last weeks. I must go."

"Of course you must. Go now. We'll see to things."

"What about Hank Teller?"

"Too hot for that lazy cur. We'll keep an eye out fer his gang. Now go with Walker to his Blue Mounds fer him to do what he has to do. Then maybe he'll settle down." She was watching the Osage packing gear on his bay and Schell's roan.

"You like him, don't you, Ruby?"

Ruby jerked her eyes back to Schell. "He's okay. Fer an Indian," she added, laughing.

Lying beside Walking Owl and listening to his even breathing, Schell smiled remembering her embarrassed response.

Ruby's assurance hadn't completely eased Schell's worries. But dozing off to sleep, he relaxed when he thought of Dee Cee's presence there.

When Cynthia left, a door closed for him—his dream ended. Without Cynthia, what was there? But today Walking Owl showed him that his dream was really just beginning. That Cynthia had been a dead-end road, just as his friend's own closed road where he couldn't find the detour.

Schell was glad he was here with Walking Owl, camping by a blackberry thicket on the edge of the wooded creek. Maybe he could help his friend find the detour. Schell slept.

Someone was shaking him. Deep in the first heavy sleep of the night, Schell had difficulty reaching consciousness. There was complete silence, no frogs, coyotes, or night birds. Rudely someone thrust his rifle in his hand and urged him to follow. Walking Owl! Instantly awake, Schell pulled on his boots and followed the wispy shadow in front of him. He dared not speak, nor did he question the

Osage's movements. Silently the two men glided through the starlit darkness, made even denser by the leafy cover of the blackberry thicket into which they crept. Ignoring the scratches to their bare hands and faces, they slithered on their stomachs through the brambles, until they found a debris-filled depression. Facing the camp which was only a few feet away, they lay prone, guns uncocked.

Too dark to see anything but the darker bulk of his friend's body, Schell could not communicate by signs. He could only touch his hand to Walking Owl's arm. Walking Owl tapped his finger against Schell's hand five distinct times.

Five men? Of course they were hostile. Friendly men would have announced their arrival long before approaching with calling out something like, "Hello, the camp." Looking at the north star's location, Schell knew that it was close to midnight. Certainly hostile. Had probably been waiting for them to go to sleep.

Schell was finally aware of the presence of the men that alerted Walking Owl. At a whistled signal, the men burst upon the friends' camp, surrounding it with shotguns and rifles leveled at their empty bedrolls.

Someone swore softly.

"They ain't here!" another said.

"I see they ain't," the leader said. "Watch your backs, men. They can't be far."

Making no effort to be quiet, the intruders tramped around the camp searching for them. Solomon's whinny from the open area where he was hobbled, told Schell that the men had their horses.

Taking advantage of the noise the men were making, Walking Owl started burrowing into the mat of leaves they were lying in. Schell did likewise. Walking Owl spread a cover over Schell, and by rolling over and back several times, covered himself.

"Okay, men, spread out," the leader said. "Search the prairie. Can't go nowhere. We've got their hosses. They're probably hidden in the tall grass."

The men lit their already prepared torches in the fire and spread out. "Watch that you don't set the grass a fire."

When the search found nothing, the leader asked, "Reckon they was dumb enough to go into the timber?"

"You know, Dick, they couldn't a-got through them briars."

"They wouldn't know that. Look anyway," Dick ordered.

With many groans and much swearing, two men stomped through the briars to the timber. With torches lighting up the area around them, they tramped back and forth among the trees.

"No sign they got this far," one called back.

"Then search the briar patch," Dick said.

One of the men, tromping down the briars to make a path as he covered the ground, reached the depression where Schell and Walking Owl lay. He paused on the higher ground, probably trying to decide whether to step into the hole. The partners, their guns ready, held their breaths, willing themselves to sink into the soft soil.

The searcher waved his torch over the hole. He paused, his boots only inches from their heads, the light from the torch sprinkled across their leaf-covered backs. Then he growled back to the leader, "They've sure vamoosed."

"Okay, come on back," Dick said, "but O'Neill, you and Hunter stay here and keep guard 'til light. We'll take their hosses and gear home and join you in the morning. Remember the signal?"

"Yeah," O'Neill grumbled as he extricated himself from the clinging briar stalks, "I remember."

Dick and the two other men headed back west from the camp, probably toward their horses, but Schell heard nothing more from that direction. At the camp, O'Neill and Hunter sat down, stoked up the fire, and chatted.

"I thought sure we had them," O'Neill said.

"Yeah. How'd you reckon they got away?"

"Must a-heerd us."

"I don't see how. I didn't even hear us and I was there."

"Don't make no sense. They couldn't a-got far."

"But they did. They ain't here."

"Well, they'll not likely come back hereabouts. We taught 'em they can't run over us."

"Yeah, we sure did."

"Lucky thing Dick spotted them."

"Yeah. Reckon they really was part of that Jesse James gang?"

"Say man, they *was* the James brothers. That tall one was Frank sure as I'm a-settin' here, and the other one with the beard, that was Jesse. No ordinary fellers coulda got away from us," Hunter said.

Schell and Walking Owl did not hear any more, for they had backed out of the hole, crawled into the timber, and rising to their feet, ran quietly northward along the creek bank, Walking Owl in the lead. After clearing earshot distance from the men at the fire, Walking Owl started down the bank to cross the creek and head east. Schell tapped him on the shoulder and pointed back the way the three men had gone.

"The odds are better now, don't you think?" he whispered.

Walking Owl straightened to his full height and let out a breath. Though Schell could not see his face in the blackness, he could visualize his friend's eyes squinting and his lips parting in anticipation when he said, "You're right. Lead on."

## Chapter Seven

Schell and Walking Owl had no trouble trailing the men who'd surprised them. Laughing and bragging about their success, the ambushers rode back down the route the friends had traveled before stopping for the night.

About a quarter of a mile behind them, Schell and Walking Owl jogged side by side down the wagon road. They felt secure in the darkness, their presence obscured by the noise of the three men who believed their prey was fleeing in the opposite direction. Safe from discovery by the black night, the partners stayed within hearing range.

Walking Owl signaled that he could circle around in front to pin them down, but Schell had a better plan. "These fellows aren't outlaws. They think we are. I don't want to start a range war in the county. I've had enough of killing."

"Whatever you say, Jesse," Walking Owl whispered back.

Schell appreciated the humor. "Those farmers won't give us a chance to explain, and even if they did, they wouldn't believe our story. Coming all this way to visit an Osage burial site! That'd be preposterous to them. They probably don't know anything about the Osage, except they are Indians and therefore prime for killing. Any explanation would put us in further danger." Schell slowed his pace as they were getting too close." He paused before he asked, "Who are the James Brothers, anyway?"

"You have been gone a long time," Walking Owl said. "They're a gang that ran with Confederate guerrillas toward the end of the war. Like Hank Teller, they have kept on—robbing trains and banks and such."

"Are they killers?"

"Yes. They robbed the bank at Liberty last February and one fellow got killed. But they're not hated like Hank Teller who goes after people in their homes. Jesse is becoming sort of a folk hero, like Robin Hood, because he steals from the wealthy. He's half feared, half respected."

"Then us being the James Brothers," Schell asked, "they'll probably not shoot us?"

"Not likely unless cornered. They could have killed us back there at camp if they'd wanted that. Bringing in Jesse and Frank James alive would be quite a coup for them. I figure that was what they were trying to do. That and the natural act of protecting their homes from killers."

The leader, Dick, pulled into the first house to an excited barking dog. "Quiet, Buck!" he ordered. Then to his companions as they continued on down the road, "Meet back here at first light." He took the lead ropes of the partners' two captured horses.

A woman in her nightgown carrying a candle threw open the door and ran out on the porch. "Dick, that you? Everything all right?"

"Yes. We're all fine." The dog continued barking. "Shut up, darn you, Buck. Go to the house."

"Here, Buck," the woman ordered. "It's only Dick." She petted the dog on the head.

"It sure enough *was* Jesse and Frank James," Dick called to her. "Gotta be. No one else would dare come here knowin' our Protection Committee is on the lookout. They got away, but we got their gear."

Stumbling in the darkness, Dick found and lit the lantern hanging by the barn door. The circle of light showed the layout of the barn. Schell and Walking Owl watched the short man dump their gear and saddles in the corner and put the horses into stalls. When Solomon snorted and flattened his ears, Dick, patted his neck. "Whoa there, boy. Easy now."

Dick stifled a yawn as he scooped out some grain for the horses from a nearby barrel before dousing the light and walking to his house.

Schell and Walking Owl crouched by the barn for an hour after the candle in the house went out. Schell touched his friend's arm. "Ready?" he whispered.

For answer, Walking Owl rose. Without making a sound, knowing exactly where to go, they entered the barn, picking up their saddles. Walking Owl's bay nickered softly in recognition as they saddled the horses and tied on their equipment.

"Anything missing?" Schell whispered.

"Don't think so."

With their hands over the horses noses to keep them quiet, they started to lead them out the door. Schell stopped, touched Walking Owl to tell him to wait, and handed him Solomon's reins. Grabbing two burlap sacks he'd noticed earlier, he dumped several scoops of grain into each sack, tied them together, and threw them over Solomon's neck. Retrieving his horse, he whispered, "Payment for our trouble."

Walking Owl chuckled.

They inched their way to the road. Their furtive movements alerted the dog, who had been sleeping by the door since Dick ordered him there. He leaped up barking, though holding his place on the porch.

Schell and Walking Owl stopped, feet in stirrups ready to mount and flee.

"Buck, shet up that noise," came a sleepy voice from inside. The dog, continued to growl deep in his throat, but lay back down obediently.

Schell and Walking Owl moved briskly past the house and down the road for about two hundred yards before mounting. This time Walking Owl led the way, heading north. Schell trusted that his friend's memory was good enough to get them safely away before light. To Schell's surprise, he headed slightly northwest, away from Blue Mounds.

Less than an hour later, they plunged into the typical wooded land which indicated a river or creek. There was just enough pre-dawn light to see that they were riding along a bluff, paralleling a river. Glints of light reflected from the water twenty feet below them. Across a bigger river than they had so far encountered, was the usual steep, black, mud bank holding at bay the wooded lowlands beyond.

"The Osage River?" Schell asked.

"The Wah-sah-she," Walking Owl agreed.

They carefully picked their way on top of the bluff near

its rim, the sound of their horses' hooves alternately crackled in the sections of dried oak leaves, clanked against the exposed sheet of rock outcroppings, and was muffled in the carpet of velvety moss. After a short distance, Walking Owl dismounted and turned left down a ravine. Carefully testing his footing and feeling his way in the early light, he led his horse to the river bank. Scanning the area, he grunted approval, turned right, and followed the river to an open area beneath an overhang.

"We'll camp here," he said.

Schell looked around him. They were in a cave-like enclosure, hidden from view in every direction except from the river itself. Even from there the opening was partially concealed by the oaks and sycamores. A grapevine, lacing through the branches, further obscured the spelean spot.

"Great!" Schell exclaimed, handing Walking Owl his reins so he could explore the cave which was about the size of a small cabin. "Here's even a place to stall the horses!" At one side were two nooks that could be turned into stalls by putting some branches at the openings.

Walking Owl grinned. "We used to camp here when trapping up the Osage River. Lots of muskrats, some otter and mink. I'd stop by here sometimes on holidays from the mission school. After we moved to Kansas, some hunting parties came back and spent a few weeks trapping along the river. They camped here to keep out of sight because the Osage weren't supposed to be in this country."

"Did you stay here the last time you came with your father?"

"Yeah. I was fifteen."

The men easily found some fallen logs to confine the horses, and unpacking their gear, they set up camp. Weary from their previous day's long journey and the night's adventures, they slept.

When Schell awakened a few hours later, Walking Owl was gone. *The man's a marvel*, he thought. *Doesn't he ever sleep?* He smelled coffee. Still warm, his meal was laid out by the embers of a fire.

Since this was Walking Owl's trip, Schell waited for his friend to say what to do next. The horses were enjoying their meal of oats, the inactivity, and the cave coolness which freed them from the flies that pestered them all the previous day. Solomon neighed softly when Schell ran his fingers through his horse's forelock and rubbed the white blaze that extended between the eyes to his nose. "Good boy," he said.

Walking Owl's bay pricked up his ears when his master appeared. While out scouting, Walking Owl had learned what their would-be captors were doing.

When Dick's companions returned at dawn and discovered the theft of the horses and gear, at first they were angry. Then they were relieved that they wouldn't have to encounter face-to-face such resourceful and dreaded men as the James Brothers. The outlaws' cleverness fit the legend told on the Missouri-Kansas border of the exploits of the elusive James Gang.

The three rode in a body to tell O'Neill and Hunter, obliterating any tracks there might have been to follow the outlaws. Not being skilled trackers, it didn't occur to them that they might have discovered at least the direction the two men took. They agreed to a man that this morning for certain the two outlaws were long gone from their neighborhood. They had thought so last night when the men were on foot, but now with their horses to speed their way, they were probably twenty miles away.

With the light of morning, O'Neill and Hunter had searched the campsite area, discovering where the friends had hidden, but lost their tracks in the woods.

Muttering among themselves, half congratulating themselves for ridding the country of the outlaws and half chagrined at how easily they were duped, the Protection Committee trooped home.

"So," Walking Owl told Schell, "if we keep out of sight, we can still do what I came here to do."

"And what exactly is that? Besides mourning at your grandfather's grave?"

"I've already done that. The larger Blue Mound, where Pawhuska is buried, is just about a mile east of us. There are houses there now, one on top of each of the mounds, like your place on Campbell's Hump. I didn't realize that the country would be so thickly settled."

"I assume no one saw you?"

Walking Owl smiled at the unnecessary question. "No one saw me. I climbed to the rock on top where Pawhuska lies. That spot is just the same."

"I know you have something else to do here. Visiting his grave wouldn't help you see your way for the future."

"In some ways it did. I've renewed my ties to this land and my Osage heritage. Watching the sun rise high in the sky from Crying Mound, I remembered my childhood here. I remembered my grandfather and what he stood for. What he did."

Walker paused, picked up a pebble and tossed it into the river. It splattered in the water, creating rings that were slowly erased by the sluggish current.

"Pawhuska saved the Osage people. What he did was not dramatic, no last-ditch stands of win or die before retreating. Nothing heroic, and stupid, like that. To survive he knew we had to cooperate with the Whites, compromise, and, yes, usually come out on the short end of the stick. But we didn't forget who we were. Our young men were not killed. We didn't waste our strength fighting an impossible fight. We are no longer the proud warriors controlling the prairies that we once were, but we are still alive, still a Nation. We are still proud, and we've retained much of what we value most."

A meadowlark called from the top of the bluff. Cicadas sang in the growing heat of the day.

"Pawhuska taught us to change. He taught that to survive with White men, we had to take on many of their ways."

"And that's okay with you?"

"Yes, but remember I've lived with White people off and on since early childhood. I see problems and advantages to both ways of living."

"So," Schell asked, "you'll now be willing to become full partner with me in the ranching business?"

Walking Owl was silent for a few seconds. He looked across the sunlit river to a huge tree leaning out over the bank. "I'm like that sycamore—leaning precariously over the never-ending flow of brown water. But I don't fall in. My roots are firmly planted in the solid, unchanging earth."

He smiled at Schell. "Yes, I'd be proud to be your partner, but I must contribute equally."

"Your expertise, your labor, your intuitive knowledge, not to mention being a crack shot, these are contributions."

"Not enough. In the White world, land is the measure of the importance of an individual. In the Osage world, land is our mother. Though the uses of the land are different in the two worlds, the end is the same. I need to own land. I've thought of that free range west of the Big Dry Wood where the McFalls have some cattle. Or the land just north of them with the river cutting through. Until I have the means to get some land, I can't be your full partner."

Schell was more perplexed than ever. "But what has our trip here got to do with that?"

"Come, I'll show you."

Securing a loaded knapsack on his back and strapping on his holster, Walking Owl led off down the bottom to where the river turned north. Carefully skirting the homesteads, they cut across the dry corn fields until they struck the river again. Following the bluff, which was almost a twin to the one where they had their camp, they dodged among the trees and brush to avoid being noticed. Overlooking the bluff stood the finest house they had yet seen. Schell searched his memory to find a name from pre-war days of anyone in the county who would have been wealthy enough to build such a house.

"Halley," Schell said to his friend. "This must be Halley's Bluff! I've heard about it, but never was here."

Walking Owl frowned. "I didn't realize there were people this close. This was our festival grounds, up there on the bluff on a large level space." He cautioned silence until they descended to the river bank. "Years ago, back in the 1790s when the Spanish claimed this land, to protect the few settlers there was a makeshift fort here called Fort Carondelet. There was no trouble with my people, and no real need for a fort. A few Frenchmen canoed up the Osage River to this place to buy our furs."

"So it was more like a trading post?"

"Earlier it was. We brought our hides and furs here. The French then stored them until the river was right to take them down to the Missouri River and on to St. Louis. Long after the fort was gone, French traders would come up the river in certain seasons to trade with us, and with White hunters, until the Civil War stopped all business."

"So what's that got to do with us?" Shell asked.

"I need to look for something here."

From the studied expression on Walking Owl's face, Schell knew his friend was finished talking. "What about the people in that house up there?"

"Complicates things," Walking Owl said. "We'll just have to be more careful."

The men climbed over fallen logs, extracted themselves from entangling vines and briars. Twice they waded through small rivulets of spring water trickling down from the bluff.

Rounding a bend, they came to a wall of rock about shoulder high above the path which was itself above the high water mark. Projecting out over the rock ledge was an overhang similar to the one at their camp only about twice as long. For about forty feet the rock ledge nestled under the protecting rock bluff. At the far end, the bluff face ended in a sloping hill that extended downstream about forty more feet and then turned to the right away from the riverbed.

Walking Owl put his hands on the ledge and jumped upon it, exclaiming, "It's just as I remembered! Only there's more dirt on top." His lips parted in pleasure.

"Keep a lookout for anyone, Schell, while I poke around here," he said. "There's not much of a place to hide if anyone from the house up there spots us."

Schell stepped out of the protecting overhang so he could see and hear if anyone approached from above. He found a lookout spot where he could also watch Walking Owl's movements. *What is the man doing*?

Walking Owl paced the area several times, studying the floor of the ledge carefully. His eyes darted from the rear of the opening to the edge, from the ceiling to the floor. Selecting a location about a foot from the edge, he knelt down and began brushing away the thin layer of loose top dirt. Then he struck the exposed rock with his knife handle. Dissatisfied with the knife, he picked up a piece of rock and continued removing the top soil and tapping the surface at six inch intervals all along the edge. When he reached the end, he moved back a few inches, and crawling back toward Schell, continued his search.

Alerted by voices, Schell whistled the bobwhite signal and dived behind a big sycamore. Walking Owl disappeared over the rock ledge.

From the top of the ravine came the sounds of horses' hooves striking against rocks. Hidden from view behind his tree, Schell heard two adolescent boys chatting. The boys passed not twenty feet from Schell's tree and, avoiding the slippery mud, led some horses to the rivulet. The boys stopped where the animals could drink without sliding down the steep muddy bank to the river.

"Reckon they're still around here?" the smaller boy asked, timidly looking about him as if expecting to see someone.

"Probably holed up under this very bluff just waitin' fer

you to come by and nab you." The smaller boy screamed when his brother grabbed him.

"Oh, leave me be."

"Scaredy-cat. Pa thinks they left and are miles off by now. They's nothin' here fer 'em, anyways. See any banks 'round here lately? The James Gang, they're after banks and sech. Probably jist a-travelin' through."

"But Dick said . . ."

"Oh, Pa says that Dick's jest imaginin' things. Him and his Protection Committee. Finding some hoss tracks leading north this-a-way provin' they's still hereabouts. Upsetting ever'body over nothin' and runnin' all over the country tellin' ever'body to arm and settin' out these patrols."

"But Pa's gonna join 'em, ain't he?"

"Yeah. All the men are for five miles around. Ain't no law in the county and we've got to do fer ourselves."

The boys returned up the hill to their house.

Schell climbed onto the rock ledge just as Walking Owl appeared. "Did you hear them?" Schell asked.

"Yeah. I guess we weren't as clever as we thought we were."

"Reckon they'll find our camp?"

"I don't know. It's well hidden. If they do, they'll sure recognize our horses, especially ole Solomon with his white face." Walking Owl looked long at the area he had been searching and said sadly, "Think we should leave?"

"Have you finished what you came for?"

"No."

"Then we can outwit that bunch of farmers. I'm with you."

Schell renewed his guard duty while his partner returned

to his search. Walking Owl's studied expression soon changed to a smile. He tapped rapidly, marking a circle about five feet in diameter. Even Schell could hear the difference in sound from the sharp crack on solid rock. This sound was duller, more muffled.

Walking Owl took from his knapsack the tarp he used to sleep on, spreading it out beside him. Then he took out a short-handled pick and shovel. With great care, cautioning Schell again to keep watch, he dug into the hard, crusted surface and removed several inches of powdery dry dirt, followed by flat sandstone rocks. He laid each rock on the tarp. Then he pulled out some logs, and still more rocks.

"Ingenious," Schell exclaimed. "No one would ever find that."

Walking Owl continued pulling out logs and rocks and carefully piling them beside him. Instead of digging into the whole five-foot marked area, he dug a deeper hole of about a foot in diameter. After about fifteen inches, he struck a different substance. Lying on his stomach, he jabbed with his knife blade at something at the bottom of his hole.

With both hands, grunting and straining, he reached into the hole. Face aglow, he pulled out a long and narrow, brown object. Schell couldn't decide which was the most handsome, Walking Owl raising to his regal height, pride and achievement both stamped on his face, or the sleek brown mink pelt he held up.

## *Chapter Eight*

"It's still in prime condition!" Walking Owl danced around the hole, holding the mink pelt above his head.

Forgetting his vigil, Schell leaped onto the ledge and took the soft pelt. He ran his hand over the velvety underfur, admiring the dark, glossy guard hairs. "This is what you came for?"

"Yes. This is my contribution, *partner*," Walking Owl's eyes danced in pleasure. He grabbed Schell's hand and pumped it, almost upsetting Schell in his enthusiasm.

"Partner? You mean it?"

Walking Owl's black eyes sparkled. "I didn't want to tell you about the cache because I didn't know if it would still be here, and after so many years, I doubted if the fur would still be good."

"It looks good to me. I assume there are more in this pit?" Schell was as excited as his friend.

"Yes," Walking Owl danced around the marked-off hole in triumph, "and there should be five more pits like this one—all here in a row. They are five feet deep."

Walking Owl knelt down by his pit and pulled out several more pelts. Some were damaged beyond use. Others were good. Sweat ran down his face as he stuffed a few good ones into his knapsack. Serious again, he began camouflaging the hole.

At Schell's questioning look, Walking Owl said, "We've got to figure out how to get these out of here without them . . ." he crooked his head toward the house on the bluff, "without attracting anyone's attention."

The sound of male voices came from the house. Walking Owl quickly covered the hole and brushed the dirt floor with a branch, obliterating the most obvious evidences of the hole and their tracks. "Not very well hidden, but perhaps no one will come here or notice."

Schell was anxious to leave as the voices at the house became louder, though they didn't come toward them. He could distinguish the sounds of horses and four or five different men. Probably the vigilante committee.

"Wait just a moment," Walking Owl whispered. "I've got one more thing to see about."

He jumped off the ledge onto the path along the river and moved downstream to the end of the bluff. On the better footing of the slope that turned away from the river, he ran easily. "If it's not fallen in, there's a tunnel just up here," he whispered to Schell who was following close behind him.

From their right through the timber, the sounds came to them clearly, unmuffled by the rock bluff barrier. Cautiously, Walking Owl sized up the terrain, and selecting a spot under a small rock outcropping, burrowed into the hillside. He reappeared almost immediately.

"It's still here. Now, let's get out of here." He started back down the river the way they had come.

Schell put out a restraining hand and pointed up the hill to the house. "First, let's eavesdrop to see what they're up to." Walking Owl grinned his agreement.

It didn't take them long to verify what they had heard from the farm boys—that the neighborhood men were organizing shifts of patrols to protect the area and search for the James Brothers. The farmers thought it would be easy to recognize the outlaws because of their horses, especially the big roan with the blaze face.

Safely away from Halley's Bluff on their way back to their camp hideout, Walking Owl told the story of the pits.

The French traders had prepared the pits in about 1812 to store the pelts the Indians brought in. Sometimes they stored them for months at a time, until they could transport them down the rivers to market in St. Louis. Just before his death, Walking Owl's father told him about his last visit to the bluff.

Though the Osage had ceded the land, they believed they still had hunting rights, and for years after they moved to Kansas, they returned to hunt and trap. They occasionally brought their furs to market at the bluff because they got a better price than selling them at the reservation trading post.

During the pre-Civil War troubles on the Missouri-Kansas border, Walking Owl's father led a small party back to the Blue Mounds region, their horses loaded with fur to trade. They found the borderland in an uproar over the raids of Abolitionists, or Free-Soilers from Kansas, and the Pro-Slavery men from Missouri.

When the Osage arrived at the bluff, they learned that some Missouri men had stopped all traffic on the big rivers. The traders could not get to the bluff on their annual buying trip. Also, the Kansans, under the leadership of John Brown, were raiding, murdering, and driving out of the area anyone with slavery sympathies. Caught in the middle of these troubles, the only recourse the Osage had was to stash their furs and flee before they became embroiled in the fight.

They cached the furs in the six rock pits and sealed them, knowing that was a safe storage place until they could return in more peaceful times. But the Civil War intervened and they never returned.

"Just before my father died," Walking Owl said, "he told me about the pelts and gave them to me. He was the only one alive of the group who cached the furs."

Knowing that Walking Owl was the last of his family, Schell asked, "How could you wait so long? They're worth a lot of money."

"Same reason as my father—no opportunity—the war, plus the restrictions on Indians traveling. After the war, I came to Independence, planning to check out my father's story. I wasn't sure just how true it was because he was in his final illness when he told me. And I figured the pelts probably would be ruined by now—they've been there for seven years. Or someone else might have found them. But when I met you, I knew that you were the key to my finding out. You know the rest."

"I'm not surprised that no one found them," Schell said. "They are hidden well. Who'd think to find anything in solid rock? You knew the pits were there, yet you had trouble locating the exact spots."

Walking Owl nodded.

"But I am surprised the pelts are in such good condition," Schell said.

"Yes, I am too, but realize, Schell, that the overhang completely blocks out the weather. The ledge is above the highest river rise, the projecting bluff keeps out any moisture, and the cave atmosphere protects it from extreme heat and cold."

"It is a perfect place."

"The French traders knew that. That is why they had those pits chiseled out, probably using Osage labor. Add to that the fact that my father knew when to trap to get the best and most durable fur, and he knew how to prepare the pelts so they would last. Some of our ceremonial robes have been handed down for generations. We know to remove all flesh and other impurities that may cause rot or decay and we know how to stretch and dry them. The pelts put into those pits were in perfect condition."

"And your father obviously knew exactly how to store the pelts for long periods of time."

"From years of experience."

"The solid rock would be a great advantage," Schell said.

"Yes, nothing could seep or crawl in. He lined the pits with large, less valuable buffalo skins before laying in the good furs."

"What about animals, insects, and other things getting in from the top?"

"You saw what I dug out of there. On top of the pelts, first more tough buffalo hides, then a layer of logs to help ventilate the hole, covered with top layers of the sandstone and dry dirt. Did you notice that on top of the whole ledge there was a layer of soil?"

"Yes."

"When I was a boy here, the rock was bare. My father put that dirt all over the top to disguise the presence of the pits. He couldn't use clay or the sandstone cement you can find around here to seal the top, because the furs have to breathe. This way he let the air filter through the loose soil and the cracks between the rocks and logs."

"What a masterly job!" Schell marveled.

In the cooler twilight they reached the bend in the river to enter their cave camp. Walking Owl said, "We've got to figure out how to reclaim and remove the furs without getting shot as outlaws or put into prison for trespassing and stealing."

Schell's mind was already busy assessing their options. They'd need help. They needed a team and wagon. Walking noiselessly ahead of his partner down the narrow path, mulling over various possibilities, but alert to any danger, he turned the last corner and stepped into the semi-dark coolness of the cave.

Sitting cross-legged in the middle of the cave and grinning broadly was a dirty frontiersman. Schell noticed his gray hair and beard, and his leather breeches and jerkin, as well as his muzzle-loading shotgun propped against a leaky canoe pulled up into the cave.

"Howdy, strangers," the man said showing toothless gums. "Been expectin' you. Mind if I set a spell?"

"You're welcome to eat with us and stay the night, friend," Schell said approaching him cautiously. Behind him Walking Owl's eyes searched the enclosure to see if there were others. When their glances met, Walking Owl silently indicated there was no one else and nothing had been disturbed.

"Silas Moore's the name. Most folks call me Si," the old man said.

Schell shook hands with him. "Schell Campbell, of near Deerfield, and this is my partner, Walker."

Walking Owl acknowledged the introduction with a nod.

"You be the fellers what spooked the farmers 'round here." Si stated. "The ones they take for Jesse and Frank James?"

Schell laughed, "I'm afraid so. They ambushed our camp near Blue Mounds last night and were impolite enough to take our gear and horses. We then paid their leader a visit in the night to get our belongings back."

Si laughed. "You should hear the stories goin' 'round about that." He clapped his hand on his leg in amusement. "One o'them farmers claimed he seen you tearin' through the night. Claims you fellers shot at him afore he shot back at you."

Schell laughed. "Nobody saw us and nobody fired a shot. Don't know why they took us for outlaws. Yesterday we rode peaceably along their roads in broad daylight. Walker here is an Osage, and he came to show his respects for his grandfather, Pawhuska, buried at Blue Mounds." There was something about this wily old man that made Schell trust him.

Si looked curiously at Walking Owl. "So you're Injun? Wouldn't have knowed it, but now you mention it, I can see it. I stayed in your village one fall years ago. Knowed your grandpap—old White Hair, they called him. Good man. Smart. Might a-knowed you, young feller, but I don't recollect no Walker."

"My Osage name is Walking Owl."

The old man's brow wrinkled in thought. "Don't rightly

recollect. That was a long time ago. Lots of little Injun young'uns."

While fixing the meal and tending to the horses, the partners discovered that Si often camped here. Tonight, it being late and his canoe leaking badly, he risked staying even though he found the spot occupied by two men he figured were the ones the country was up in arms about. One look at the brand on their horses and their spartan gear told him they were not the notorious James Brothers who always rode first class, never holing up in caves despite the stories. Si indicated that he was about at the end of his rope, his canoe past repair, his traps mostly lost, and the catch poor.

While the men visited and attended to camp duties, Schell was forming a plan to remove the furs. Si's presence gave him the piece to the problem he was missing. After Si bedded down for the night, Schell whispered to Walking Owl, "I've got a plan. I'll work on it during my watch and tell you in the morning."

Walking Owl nodded, lay down on his blanket, and was almost instantly asleep in the coolness of the cave.

In spite of the lingering heat of the day, Schell moved close to the embers of the fire, put on a few sticks, took paper and pen from his knapsack and began to write, ignoring the bats that darted over the river catching insects.

Next morning before dawn, while drinking the strong coffee, Schell asked their visitor, "Si, how'd you like to go to work for Walker and me?"

Surprised, Si choked. It was a few minutes until he got his throat cleared to talk. "Don't know how you could use an old codger like me?"

"Walker and me, we've got a big spread and are looking

toward doubling it this fall. We're into cattle—maybe even sheep later. Now the trouble is there are lots of coyotes and wolves, bobcats, and other animals that are getting to the calves and generally keeping the herd riled up. We can't even think of getting sheep because of having to watch them so close."

He winked at Walking Owl to let him know this was part of his plan, though his partner did not have a clue where this was going.

"Now, it occurred to me last night after listening to your recent setbacks, that you would be just the person to rid our ranch of these varmints."

Si sat up straighter, a smile showing through the bushy hair on his face. His bright eyes darted from Schell to Walking Owl.

"What do you think?" Schell asked.

"I think I ain't never heard of no Injun partner afore."

"Well, you have now. What do you think about the job? We want you to start right away, today, in fact. With this dry weather the coyotes are getting bold."

The partners looked at Si, waiting for him to answer. Walking Owl's puzzled expression was gone. He had figured out that this was Schell's way to get a message home for the help they needed.

When Si didn't answer, Walking Owl said, "You'll like it there for it's like this country. There's a small river nearby. We've got a bunkhouse on the ranch where you can stay. The ranch buildings are on a mound like these around here."

"What's the pay?" Si asked.

"Board and ten dollars a month."

"And you can have all the skins you trap on the ranch," Walking Owl said.

"You got you a hand." Si held out his open palm to finalize the deal. Schell shook it. "I'm ready to go. My canoe is ruint. All I've got is jest my gear here," he motioned to his ancient knapsack and bedroll. "Only I ain't got no horse."

"Take mine," Schell said, leading out the roan. "Only keep off the roads until you get several miles from here, because these farmers will recognize Solomon's blaze face."

"Ain't got no cause to worry on my account. I ain't fixin' to be taken fer one of them James Boys." Si laughed at the joke of anyone mistaking a grizzly old man like him for the young handsome outlaws. He jumped up, looking ten years younger. Walking Owl saddled Solomon, while Si gathered his few belongings and tied them to the saddle. "But what about you? How're you gonna git home if I take yer hoss?"

Schell handed him a letter. "Give this letter to either my sister Martha or to Dee Cee McFall who is staying with her. I'm asking her to send a neighbor boy back here with my mules and wagon. We've got some ranch business to attend to hereabouts and supplies we need to haul back."

Si stuck the letter into an inner pocket of his jerkin.

"Can you read?" Schell asked.

"No."

"Do not give this letter to anyone else, do you understand?" Si nodded. "Solomon can get you there tonight, so keep riding even if it is late."

"What'll I tell them at yer ranch 'bout you fellers?"

"Whatever anyone asks you. I've written what I want done in the letter."

Schell then gave him directions to Campbell's Hump, told him to get to work right away on the wolves, and sent him on his way.

Walking Owl looked at Schell with admiration. He laughed with him over the exaggerated danger of wolves. "What did you say in your letter?"

Schell smiled. "I worked on it a long time last night. I didn't want anyone else who might read it to figure out what we're doing, but I wanted Dee Cee and Martha to understand the urgency and act immediately, yet not be worried. This is what I wrote:

> *Blue Mounds*
> *July 6, 1866*
>
> *My Dear Sister Martha and Friend Dee Cee,*
>
> *I trust you are well as are both of us. Please put this man in the bunkhouse. I have hired him to kill the wolves, but don't worry about him. He knows what to do.*
>
> *Walker has some good news, but we need the team and wagon to complete our business. So, I'm asking you to prepare the wagon, put on the covered top, and pack enough supplies for three days. Get Red to drive it to us. It is essential that he leaves tomorrow morning very early. Have him stop in Nevada City at the mercantile, where I have an account, to bring the supplies I've listed on the back. I've also written the directions where he is to go when he gets here.*
>
> *He is not to mention my name or his real purpose in being here, as we have run into some local diffi-*

*culties. The old man will tell you about it. Red can
make up some story to explain his presence. I want
him to stop at this particular homestead, asking permission to spend the night. He is to act normal and
set up camp. We will find him after dark.*

*I am your devoted brother and friend, hoping to
return home the next day after the wagon arrives.*

Walking Owl congratulated him. "Well done. Dee Cee
will know what to do. What about the boy? Can Red do
it on his own?"

"Yeah. Dee Cee and Ruby will coach him what to do
and say when he gets here. Until then, we might as well
take it easy."

Walking Owl shook his head. "Not yet. We need to
move those furs to a place where we can quickly load the
wagon."

"I'm working on that problem. Got any ideas?"

"Yes. Remember that opening I found in the hillside
yesterday?"

"Uh-huh."

"Well, it goes back in the hill far enough to hold all the
furs. I remember it because we kids used to play in there
some. It is an old exploratory mining tunnel the French
had dug years ago. They didn't find the gold, silver, or
lead they were looking for."

"Great! It would be easier to load from there, too."
Schell laughed.

"What's so funny?" Walking Owl asked.

"The directions to the farm that I gave to Red were to
Halley's Bluff."

"And from that tunnel it's only a few rods to the old

ceremonial grounds beside the house where he could camp?"

"Exactly. That's where I told him to stay the night."

"So, let's get busy." Walking Owl buckled on his holster, slung his rifle by its strap across his back, and picked up his knapsack. "If we're to move all those furs under the noses of the people on the bluff, we better get at it."

Walking Owl fed his horse while Schell hid their gear and erased the evidence of their camp in case someone not as friendly as Si, should find it.

For the next two days, with one keeping watch, the other dug out of the pits as many furs as he could carry at a time to the tunnel. The furs in the two pits on the ends were completely ruined. In one of the pits, several pelts at the top and around the edges were damaged, but they recovered a wagon load of good furs, mostly beaver.

After emptying each pit, the men refilled it with rocks and driftwood, covering the top with dirt. Their purpose was temporary concealment in case someone happened down that way before they left. Once they were gone, they did not care if anyone discovered the pits.

The work was slow and stressful. Twice each day the boys from the house brought the horses to water, but they did not even glance downstream to the overhang. The extreme heat during midday convinced Walker and Schell that they should concentrate their efforts early and late. Working during the night was too difficult, because without a light, they stumbled, stepped on sticks, and otherwise made noises that might reveal their presence.

By early evening of the second day, the partners had stacked all the good furs in the tunnel. They made sure that the rock ledge gave no evidence of their work. They crouched in the brush near the tunnel watching and listening for any sign of Red arriving with Schell's wagon. Though the cover was sparse near the tunnel, they risked staying there. They could see the path leading to the homestead; they could hear most sounds in the trail in front of the house.

Squatting in the mouth of the tunnel, Schell kept rubbing his hands together and stroking his beard. Walking Owl had difficulty maintaining his usual calm demeanor. He alternately peered up the hill toward the house and sat down, arms crossed on his chest.

"Shouldn't have given the boy a man's job," the Osage mumbled.

Schell agreed. "We shouldn't have involved the McFalls in this." Equally worried, he was having second thoughts. He raised up, bumped his head on the low tunnel ceiling, and with a soft oath, crouched down again.

"What if Red gets hurt?" he worried.

"If anything happened to him, Ruby would never forgive us," Walking Owl said. "She's already lost more than most women could bear."

"Right."

The men sat in uncomfortable silence for several minutes.

Suddenly from the trail on the far side of the farmhouse, sounded a faint call of a whippoorwill. The friends jerked up, looking at each other as if to ascertain the voice was human. After a pause there was another call, slightly closer.

"Red!" Schell exclaimed. "That's his all safe signal."

With his ear to the ground to hear the vibrations, Walking Owl agreed. "Team and wagon," he said catching his breath.

Schell soon heard the rumble of the wagon and the crack of the mules' shoes on the rocks.

"Hello, the house," called a faint voice from the direction of the wagon which was still hidden from the men's view.

"Hello, the house," came louder and more insistent.

"That's not Red," Walking Owl's whisper quavered. "That's Ruby's voice!"

A woman, the two boys Schell had seen, and some smaller children spilled out of the house. The woman held a shotgun, shading her eyes against the setting sun to see who was coming.

"Who's there?" she called.

The hidden men saw the team and the canvas-covered wagon pull over the rise. To their horror they recognized Martha beside Ruby on the wagon seat. Dee Cee, dressed as usual in male clothing, with her hat pulled down to her eyes, rode beside the wagon on her pony.

Schell trembled in anger at Dee Cee for ignoring his orders and putting Martha, and Ruby, not to mention herself, in great danger. Instead of bringing the help he wanted, here she had compounded the problem by adding more people to protect; maybe jeopardized the whole project.

"Speak up," the woman repeated, pointing the gun at them, "Who's there?"

"Ruby McFall from near Deerfield. Is this here the road to the ferry across the river?"

"No, you missed it. Back about five miles."

"Oh dear, oh dear me! So far?" Ruby's consternation

increased. "I don't know what to do. And night comin' on and we're supposed to be 'cross the river by now. Oh dear! Lost our way!"

Almost ready to cry, Martha clung to Ruby. Dee Cee reined her pony beside Ruby, looking around her with frightened eyes.

"Ma, what'll we do?" she asked fearfully.

On the verge of tears, Ruby looked at the fine house and open lawn as if seeing them for the first time. "Can my young'uns and me rest the night here? We come the whole way today and the mules is about tuckered out what with the heat and fightin' the flies."

In truth the mules did look spent. White foamy lather spilled out from under their collars down their necks, and their heads drooped as they stood motionless except for their swishing tails.

"And we heerd they's outlaws about," Ruby continued fearfully. "Without my man I'm scared of campin' out alone on the road with nobody but these young'uns."

The farm woman lowered her gun.

"I'd be mighty obliged to you if you'd let us stop jest fer tonight," Ruby begged.

"Where's your man?"

"Over to Appleton City. We're goin' to him."

Dee Cee gave the woman an imploring glance, though the watching men noticed that she was scanning the area.

"They're wonderful," Walking Owl whispered, and then startled Schell by giving a loud whippoorwill call.

Dee Cee smiled. Martha grabbed Ruby's hand. To prevent the farm woman from seeing the joy in the child's face, Ruby drew Martha to her, pushing her face against her ample breast. On cue, Martha started crying.

"See, lady, how wore out my girl is. She's sickly and I don't think she can go no farther. Ask your man if it's all right."

"He ain't here. He's out gallivantin' over the country chasin' outlaws."

Martha cried out and clasped Ruby.

"There, there, dearie," Ruby said patting her. "we're safe now. The outlaws wouldn't come here."

The farm woman, followed by her boys, walked up to the wagon, looked into the back, studied Dee Cee and the weeping Martha, and said, "I reckon you can stop, but my man won't like it. Pull up over there." She pointed to an open area back the way they'd come.

When Ruby started to turn the mules around, Walking Owl gave the whippoorwill call several more times.

"Ma," Dee Cee said, "That spot over there, that level spot in the edge of the trees, that looks like a good cool place. We'd be less bother to these good folks there, and we could water the team down to the river from there."

Ruby looked at the woman for her permission. "Go ahead," the woman said. "Will you need anything?"

"Thank you no. We've got ever'thing. May need to wash this dust off'n us at the river."

"All right. There's a path down to the river jest behind that big maple there."

The woman returned to the house. The children watched Ruby cluck to the mules to urge them to move and then pull them to a stop about three hundred feet from the house in the spot that Dee Cee indicated.

Martha jerked out of Ruby's clasp and clapped her hands in glee, before Ruby's restraining hand cautioned her to keep quiet a bit longer. The woman called the children to the house.

When the coast was clear, Dee Cee let out her breath. "We done it."

Martha was eagerly looking about her. "Schell is here. I heard his whistle. Why doesn't he show himself?"

"Jest be patient, dearie," Ruby said, securing the reins and collecting her skirts to climb down from the wagon. "He'll come when it is safe and then he'll . . ."

Schell appeared beside the wagon on the blind side from the house. He pulled Martha from the high seat and hugged her, while putting his finger to his mouth to warn her to stay quiet. He finished Ruby's sentence, "And then he'll say that Martha is a good pretend weeper, that Ruby is the biggest liar he ever heard, and that Dee Cee," he put out his hand to grab Dee Cee who had dismounted and walked to the wagon. He looked sternly at her, his anger softening as he saw the determined tilt of her head and set lips. "And that Dee Cee disobeys orders endangering the three women who mean the most to me in the whole world."

## Chapter Nine

Dee Cee jerked her arm away from his grasp. "Since when do you give me orders?"

"It wasn't all Dee Cee's doings, Schell," Ruby said.

"No," Martha said, "Ruby and I made her take us."

"But I wanted Red . . ."

Walking Owl stepped behind Schell, raised his hat to Ruby, smiled at Dee Cee and Martha, and said quietly. "We'll work this out later. You ladies were superb! But you better set up camp before that woman gets suspicious."

"Right," Schell said. "Be sure one of you watches the house at all times."

"I guess we know what to do," Dee Cee retorted.

Walking Owl said to Ruby, "We're just under the hill down there. Don't come to us, we'll come to you."

Ruby nodded.

"What's this all about?" Dee Cee asked, looking first at Schell, then at Walking Owl. "I understand why you are hiding, but what's Walker's good news you wrote about?"

Just then the biggest boy came out of the house carrying

a covered pan. The men faded into the dusk as the boy approached the women.

"Ma sent you some hot stew. Thought it would help you out after your long trip."

"Oh, how thoughtful! Tell yer Ma thanks." Ruby looked into the pot. "Look, kids, here's enough for our suppers. Thank goodness, Dee Cee, you don't have to build a fire in this heat."

"Yeah, Ma. Marthie and I'll jest water my pony and the mules down to the river afore we eat," she said.

"I'll show you," the boy said. "I do it all the time, only I go down the trail up by the house. But see, there's a path down here, too." He took the lead rope of one of the mules to show the way. Dee Cee and Martha followed. Not twelve feet from where they passed, Schell and Walking Owl hunched over in the mouth of the tunnel.

The boy chatted about the exciting news of the neighborhood—the James Brothers and his father's part in tracking them down.

"Them outlaws stole some hosses jest south of here a ways," he said.

"Oh, they did?"

"Yeah. And most likely holed up somewheres 'round here." He spoke in almost a whisper, looking about him as if the noted criminals were within earshot. "Dick says they's out to git all our hosses."

"I thought Jesse James robbed banks and trains," Dee Cee said, pretending to be equally impressed with the enormity of the possibility.

"Naw. They're after anything. And will shoot you jest as soon as look at you."

"Will your Pa be back soon," Dee Cee asked in a trembling voice. "Ma and Marthie and me, we'd sure feel lots safer if he was here."

"He has the first watch," the boy said proudly. "He's out patrollin' 'til midnight. People are scared to git out on the roads. You're sure brave."

"Just plain ignorant," Dee Cee said. "We didn't know nothin' about them until a farmer down the road told us." She looked around pretending to see danger behind each tree. "Don't know what we'd a-done tonight if your ma hadn't let us stay." She shuttered at the thought of being alone with such men on the loose.

After they returned to the wagon, the boy's mother called him to the house.

After dark when the real whippoorwills were calling, Schell and Walking Owl appeared, each carrying a load of furs. "Stay in the wagon as if you've gone to bed," Schell whispered. Everyone piled into the back of the wagon, closing the flap.

Ruby and Dee Cee exclaimed over the furs while the men told their story.

"Quick, now," Schell said, "we've got to hustle before morning. Martha," he ordered, unconsciously assuming his lieutenant tone, "you sit here by the front flap and watch for anyone, especially the man, returning. Keep your ears peeled."

"You don't need to tell her," Dee Cee snapped at him. "She knows what to do."

Schell's heart yearned toward his little sister who had to learn these war survival tactics so young.

Ruby was spreading out the furs in layers on the floor of the wagon. "I'll keep 'em hidden with this canvas you asked us to git in Nevada City," she said. "Now I know why you wanted it."

"I'll help you fellers," Dee Cee announced, slipping out the back of the wagon. She followed the men down the slope to the tunnel.

Walking Owl's gentle touch on Schell's arm caused him to choke back another order for her to stay put. Having two women and a child in his command was almost more than he could handle. But Walker seemed to welcome their presence, and he reminded himself, this was Walker's operation. Schell had never known the Osage's instincts to be wrong. He swallowed his pride and curbed his natural impulse to protect women; he knew he had to accept these women as equals.

As they worked, out of sight and earshot of the house, either in the wagon or in the tunnel, the men learned that when Dee Cee heard Martha read the letter and found out from Si about the fix the men were in, she decided that she, not Red, was the one who should return with the wagon. Martha, as determined and independent as Dee Cee, absolutely refused to be left home. If there was something she could do to help, she vowed she would never again stay safe while her family was in danger.

After making their plans, the girls rode over to Ruby's house to tell her and get one of the boys to stay with Si at The Hump. Agreeing that Dee Cee should go instead of Red, Ruby did not even object to Martha's accompanying her. Then she surprised all of them by announcing that she would go too. Ruby, like Martha, was tired of staying home worrying about her family. This was a job women could do, and do probably better than men. Schell and Walking Owl, the best friends her family had known since old Sam Campbell's death, needed her help in a dangerous venture. No argument from Dee Cee or her sons could dissuade her.

Before light the next morning, after pumping from Si all he could tell them about the men and the area, the three women pulled out. Though the dog Harris was determined to follow, everyone agreed that he should stay on The Hump. Two boys and an untried old man needed his help to guard both places. Red tied him up until the wagon was out of sight.

At their campsite in the darkness under the wagon top, Ruby's excitement increased with each new load of furs that she packed. "I've not seen pelts this good for years. Walker, I know jest the man in Ft. Scott to take them to."

Though she could not see Walking Owl's face, she knew he valued her opinion since the McFalls had survived the war years by trapping. She added, "If we handle things right, you could git you a ranch with these."

"First we got to get them out of here," Schell cautioned.

Dee Cee said very little while she kept pace with the men trip for trip. Schell was quiet, still angry that she'd allowed Martha to come. Bad enough that the two women came, but how could she put a little girl in this danger! Ruby and Walking Owl chatted in a guarded undertone during each trip to the wagon.

While Schell and Dee Cee were stowing into the wagon some of the last furs, from her perch on the wagon seat, Martha gave one hoot owl call—the night warning signal. After a pause she repeated it. The man returning? Dee Cee dived into the back, pulling Schell in after her. Half way to the wagon and bent under his load of furs, Walking Owl swiftly retreated and squatted in the black tunnel.

Dee Cee and Ruby jerked aside some heavy pelts. Schell slipped under them. Martha crawled under the wagon cover through the front flap. The women quickly spread the canvas over the furs and scattered their bedding and belongings over all. They were ready to lie down on top of the buried Schell as if asleep.

They heard the regular rhythm of a trotting horse approach the gate area and then stop. Peering through the front flap, they saw a light go on in the house, revealing a man dismounting. There were voices and activity around the barn. The man entered the house, but after a few minutes burst out the door again carrying a lantern, followed by his wife in her long night dress. As they drew nearer the wagon, the woman begged, "Bill, don't wake 'em in the middle of the night. You'll scare 'em. I tell you it's jest a woman and two young'uns. She got lost. What was I to do, send 'em out fer them outlaws to murder?"

"Woman, ain't you got no sense at all?" the man asked.

Ruby poked her head out the front flap and asked sleepily, "Is somethin' wrong?"

Bill stopped short, held up his lantern to see better. Satisfied that Ruby was really a middle-aged woman, he strode all around the wagon. "Lots of tracks here leading down to the river."

"Of course they is, Bill. I told you they's three of them with two mules and a horse. Billy helped them water the stock in the river."

Ruby repeated, "Is somethin' the matter?"

"Mighty strange you comin' up our lane jest now," the man growled.

Dee Cee joined Ruby at the flap. Martha, holding tight

to Ruby, started crying and screaming, "Ma, don't let the outlaws get me."

"He ain't no outlaw, dearie," Ruby said, hugging the frightened child to her. "He's the man what lives here."

"Don't be such a big cry–baby," Dee Cee said. "He ain't gonna hurt you."

Bill had backed off the minute Martha started bawling. "Didn't mean no harm, lady. Jest checkin'."

"I can understand that, but do you need to scare us, wakin' us up like this in the middle of the night? We're jest a-passin' through. Yer woman was kind enough to let us stay the night. We'll be gone afore first light in the mornin'."

"They missed the road to the ferry," the woman explained, trying to pull him back to the house.

"Yeah," Dee Cee said, "we're on our way to Pa in Appleton City."

"It's okay, dearie," Ruby said to Martha who was still weeping. "Now, be a big girl and go on back and lay down." Martha lay on top of the furs covering Schell. She pulled a light comforter over her, spreading it out.

Bill held the lantern up to the front flap close to Ruby and Dee Cee, studying them. "Mind if I look inside?"

The woman was angry. "Why on earth for, Bill. Ain't you got no neighborliness left in you?"

Ruby pulled back the flap. "I don't mind. Jest our beds and gear for travelin'." She fumbled behind her and handed the woman the pot. "Oh, and here, Ma'am, is yer pot all washed up fer you. Thank you kindly for the supper last night."

Even though outflanked by Ruby and his wife, Bill marched around to the back, pulled aside the flap and held up his lantern to see inside. The lantern illuminated the interior. His wife stuck her head in beside his. "See what'd I tell you? Nothin' but the little girl and sleepin' stuff."

Bill had one foot up ready to climb in when one of the mules whinnied softly from down the slope where they were hobbled. Leaving the wagon, but still not completely satisfied, Bill tromped to the horses, held up his lantern to see, and said, as if disappointed, "Just a pair of mules and a pinto pony."

"Yes, what'd you expect?" the woman asked.

"The James Brothers rode a bay and a roan with a blaze face. These ain't them."

" 'Course they ain't."

Grumbling, Bill returned to the wagon without noticing Walking Owl who had moved from tree to tree closer to the wagon in case Ruby couldn't handle the farmer. Bill wished them a curt good night and strode back to his house.

"Don't mind him," the wife said. "All this Jesse James stuff and the Protection Committee patrols is makin' him edgy."

"We'll be gone in the mornin'," Ruby said. "We're obliged to you."

Half an hour later the lights in the house went out. Schell, wet-through with perspiration and almost smothered under the weight of the furs and Martha's body, slipped out of the wagon to give the all clear to Walking Owl. The men waited another half hour before bringing in the final load.

Ruby pushed aside the bedding, clothing, and camping items she had scattered over the canvas tarps. Under them was a foundation of pelts stacked on the wagon floor.

Bill's cursory examination did not reveal that the bedding was almost level with the tops of the wooden sides of the wagon bed.

With the furs safely loaded and the tunnel entrance hidden again with brush, the five people held a quick conference in the blackness of the covered wagon. Getting the wagon and women back down the road out of the danger area posed no problem. Ruby and the girls would simply retrace their steps to the turnoff they supposedly missed to get to the ferry to Appleton City. Their greatest danger (since they wouldn't turn toward the ferry) would be in the stretch right after the ferry road until they drew near Nevada City. But they gambled that the road crossing was far enough away from the Blue Mounds area to outdistance the suspicion of anyone who might have noticed them the day before.

"We can take care of ourselves if anyone does git suspicious," Dee Cee said, annoyed at Schell's fussing over them.

"Yes," Walking Owl said, "you and Ruby, and little Martha here, I'm sure you can. Right, Schell?"

Reluctantly, remembering how convincing their act was with the farmer and his wife, Schell had to agree.

The main problem was how to get the two men back home since Si had taken Schell's horse. For one of them to use Dee Cee's pinto was out of the question because their hosts, or someone on the women's route as they retraced their steps, might become suspicious about the missing pony.

They devised a plan. Since Walking Owl looked less like one of the James brothers than Schell, and since the furs were his to safeguard, he would meet the wagon in the morning at a spot on the road near the men's cave-camp. From then on he would ride in the wagon, remaining hidden in the back until they were well on the way. After leaving the Blue Mounds region, he could drive the team. People they met on the way would assume he was the head of the family.

Schell would leave immediately riding Walking Owl's bay across country as far as he could get before light. Safely away, he would try to intercept the wagon in Nevada City, but failing that, he would see them all again the following evening at Campbell's Hump.

Schell hugged Martha and Ruby and started to hug Dee Cee. She held out her hand to him instead. Walking Owl described to Ruby and Dee Cee the place for the meeting in the morning and murmured a soft, "See you ladies tomorrow." The men melted into the night, finding their way cautiously and slowly to their cave bluff up the Osage River. Several times Walking Owl had to urge Schell on and reconvince him that their plan was a good one. Schell's instincts kept telling him to return to protect the women.

"They are survivors, my friend," Walking Owl said. "This job is nothing compared to what they've been doing for years."

Schell pictured Cynthia and the women he'd known in the East. Not the same at all. Walker was right. This would be child's play for his western women.

At noon the next day, Schell was in Nevada City. Since he knew that his partner and the women could not get there for at least a couple of hours, he decided to tend to some business. That would help him pass the time and ease his anxiety. Giving a kid a nickel to tell him when his wagon arrived, Schell made some purchases at the mercantile, where he learned that the bank would soon reopen. The town was reviving.

He picked up a month-old issue of the new newspaper, the *Nevada City Times*, dated June 16, 1866. The front page carried details of the bank robbery by the James-Younger Gang back in February at Liberty, up near Kansas City. *Old news*, Schell thought, but since this was the first newspaper printed since the town burned, it was news to the townspeople. The article warned people in western Missouri to look out for these bandits. "Bold and daring," the article said, "the James Brothers ride openly on fine horses. Frank, the elder and taller of the two often rides a bay stallion."

Schell finally understood why he and Walking Owl had caused such suspicion.

Cramming the paper into one of his saddlebags, he then went to the office of the one lawyer in town to initiate legal proceedings on his father's estate. He accompanied the lawyer to the makeshift courthouse. Only since January had the county's official business been conducted in the burned-out county seat. The two men conferred with the public administrator, who was trying to untangle the mess the records were in since nothing had been recorded during the war years. The Campbell records were in order, needing only payment of back taxes. Schell paid the taxes and the fees to have the titles transferred to himself.

While there Schell learned that some of the land that Walking Owl was interested in obtaining was still public land. Good, Walker could buy it. Knowing that Mac

McFall claimed the river bottom and some prairie acreage, Schell searched for those records.

None. There were no records that Mac had filed or owned so much as an acre! Some land speculator from the East claimed most of the land in the river bottom.

Schell, his business concluded, sat on a log in the shade of a cottonwood greatly perturbed about the McFall land. Leaves rustled in the hot southwest wind. Expecting his wagon at any moment, he shaded his eyes to peer up the dusty Main Street that formed the west side of the once-busy square. There were several riders and people walking, but no wagon as far as he could see across the patches of cultivated land and open prairie.

He must talk to Ruby. After their years-long struggle to hold on to their home, the McFalls had nothing! He couldn't imagine Ruby letting that happen. She was too smart. Then he realized he was thinking of her as a man. It was different for a woman. There was the old state law that allowed only heads of households—men, not women—to file and own land. Men took care of business deals like buying land. Rarely was the wife's name on the deed. In fact, the record of the deed to Campbell's Hump he'd just seen in the county records did not include his mother's name. He determined right then to add Martha's name to his on the new deed when it was processed.

And Ruby, handicapped even more by not being able to read, had no way of knowing that she and her sons—he caught himself—her *children* owned nothing.

He was surprised at himself, thinking only of the McFall men. How could he ignore Dee Cee? No one had done more to safeguard the McFall family than she. He visualized her pert expression, her auburn head held high, her never-still blue eyes seeing everything around her. He smiled. Strange woman. Ever since he discovered she was a girl, he had been unconsciously comparing her to Cynthia—his model of the epitome of womanhood. In comparison, Dee Cee had always failed badly.

He had never met a woman like her. His own mother was a frontierswoman who often did a man's work, but she was first and foremost a woman. Even Ruby, hearty, rough, and bold as she was, filled well his idea of a woman.

Not Dee Cee.

He smiled. Yet she had qualities the other women he knew lacked. She was independent, outspoken, athletic, an excellent shot, a forceful leader, as well as smart, brave, resourceful, ready, quick, dependable, agile, strong. He could go on. Then he realized these were the qualities he looked for in a man—qualities he wanted in a partner. Abilities equal to his, like Walking Owl possessed.

Was the reason he felt antagonistic to her because she was as capable as he? And did she not warm up to his feeble efforts to be more friendly because he was not treating her as an equal, but as a dependent woman?

He had to admit that Dee Cee had been right about this trip to Blue Mounds. Walking Owl recognized that right away. Of course she was the better person to bring him his wagon than her youthful brother. Red couldn't have talked his way through like the two woman and Martha did. His story wouldn't have been convincing, and he'd have used his gun when things got sticky. But the women, Dee Cee, Ruby, and Martha, played their roles perfectly. They succeeded in doing what Schell wanted by *not* following his orders. All of them independent women. Even little Martha. He smiled at how his sister's quick play-acting at crucial moments may have prevented their discovery, how her body on his had protected him from discovery.

Schell tried to remember his behavior toward Dee Cee. When he first returned to The Hump, thinking she was a man, he admired her skill, quickness, and nerve. And after he found out she was a girl? He admitted that he felt betrayed, cheated. Maybe even humiliated? He had resented her deception. But in truth, she hadn't tried to deceive him. Never did she or any of the McFalls say she was a man. He just assumed it because she was doing a man's job. It wasn't her fault he was blinded by gender role bias. Walking Owl wasn't deceived.

Schell grinned. She wasn't filling any role, either male or female. She was simply Dee Cee. She was living, working, and protecting her family in the way she could. He remembered the admiration that he first felt toward her when she and her brothers had pinned down him and Walking Owl, two experienced frontiersmen and soldiers. She was doing what everyone in this war-ravaged country was doing—surviving and rebuilding.

The lookout boy ran up to him, pointing north. "There's yer wagon, mister."

Schell jumped up, trembling with relief. They made it! He vaulted on the bay and stirring up a cloud of dust, galloped the few blocks to meet them. In the middle of the dirt street, they openly greeted one another. Schell hugged Martha and Ruby. Dee Cee stayed aloof, but smiled as she was glad to see him.

"How'd it go?" he asked Walking Owl who was driving the mules with Ruby beside him.

"Smooth as silk."

Martha climbed on the bay behind Schell, full of the story, speaking rapidly.

"We left before light, even before the people in the house had got up. But when we passed the door, Ruby called out thanks to them. We thought Walker had missed us, but then he scared us by jumping into the wagon when we turned at one of those right angle turns. Even Dee Cee didn't see him. He stayed in the back for a few miles. Nobody saw us until we got to a farm on the road where a dog barked and a man his wife called Dick ran out to us. Ruby pulled up, explained we had missed the ferry turn, got directions, and drove on."

Schell and Walking Owl exchanged grins.

"After that Walker got up front and we just rode on in to town like ordinary people. Then we saw you. Oh, Schell, wasn't it all wonderful? Ruby, Dee Cee, Walker. Aren't they wonderful? Wasn't I wonderful?"

Schell laughed, "Yes, Martha, you all are. Truly wonderful." He looked at Dee Cee riding her pinto beside them. "Dee Cee," he said, "I'm glad you came instead of Red. You were right. Red couldn't have pulled it off."

Dee Cee smiled back. Schell couldn't remember her smiling at him like that before. Her eyes sparkled under the upswept auburn lashes.

"Don't mention it," she said. "Nothin' to it. Glad to help Walker out." The three of them turned to look at Walking Owl and Ruby sitting close together on the wagon seat. They all laughed.

"How about some candy at the mercantile?" Schell asked Martha. "Everyone come on in. This calls for a celebration. Let's get some cheese and crackers, pickles, and whatever else they've got we can eat here."

Laughing and chatting noisily in relief from the tension of the past few days, the group trooped into the general store. No need to pretend anymore as they were in their home town where people knew them.

"My treat," Walking Owl said. No one objected.

They were enjoying their snack in the shade of the store front, when a hot, dusty rider arriving from the northeast pulled up. Excited, he ran into the store, "Hey, ever'body, them James Brothers were spotted over to Blue Mounds. That whole country is out lookin' fer them. They say. . . ."

## Chapter Ten

"Please, Schell," Martha begged at the dinner table "let's go to the preaching at Deerfield. There's not much to do around here now. We can't do anything about Walker's land until the lawyer man in town gets the papers all in order."

Schell and Walking Owl were resting a few minutes after the noon meal before returning to work. Si had already left the table. The partners smiled at Martha's eagerness and naivety. Everywhere they looked was work to be done, even on The Hump, not counting what they wanted to do on Walking Owl's new land. True, the final papers were not signed, but the lawyer assured them there would be no problem.

There were the new cattle Walking Owl bought the week before in Ft. Scott when he sold his wagon-load of furs for $1,000.00—a virtual fortune. Fur prices were high after the scarcity of the war years. Unable to tolerate the hot, dry weather, a rancher who was moving back east sold Walking Owl his herd at a bargain. The partners drove the cattle to The Hump to range with Schell's, almost doubling their herd.

Their next trip was to the Nevada City land office. They learned that Walking Owl was eligible to file for 160 acres under the Homestead Act. Any man serving honorable time in the United States Army could file. That stipulation qualified Walking Owl, for normally Indians could not own land outside their reservations.

"Name," the land agent had asked when filling out the government forms.

"Walking Owl."

The agent grumbled, "What kind of name is that?"

Schell answered, "Walker. Put down 'Walker.' "

The agent wrote that down, then asked, "First name?"

Walking Owl grinned at Schell, "Frank," he said. "Frank is a good name, don't you think, Jesse?" The agent stared at the two men as if they were crazy. They were both laughing and slapping each other on the shoulders.

"Frank Walker, one hundred and sixty acres," he wrote down.

After that they visited the lawyer to have him contact the eastern landowners of tracts of land near them to see if they would sell.

Not much to do! Schell laughed at Martha. "Well, Sis, I guess we can take off Sunday to take you to the meeting."

Martha clapped her hands. "Oh, thank you. The McFalls are going, too. I'll just ride over there and tell them we'll all go together in our wagon." She ran out the door for her pony without waiting for Schell's approval.

"Si," she called to the old man as she mounted. "We're going to the meeting tomorrow. You coming?"

"Not me," Si said. "No meetin' fer me. I'm too far gone fer redemption."

"You coming with us?" Schell asked Walking Owl. "Si and ole Harris can watch the place if you want to go." With no further trouble from outlaws, he hoped that things were getting back to normal times again.

Walking Owl hesitated before nodding. He wouldn't attend the services, Schell knew, but he always seemed to enjoy an outing. "Reckon it's a good idea for everyone to be gone?" he asked.

"We'll just be gone for the day. Yeah, I think it's safe enough now. We need a holiday, and I'm sure some good church-going wouldn't hurt an old sinner like me."

After doing the morning chores and giving Si instructions for the day, Schell, handsome in his dark suit and white shirt, climbed up to the wagon seat and took the reins. Beside him sat Walking Owl, as usual in his old army pants but sporting a new blue chambray shirt. Martha, proudly wearing the new dress Ruby made for her from the printed calico material Schell bought in Ft. Scott. Schell drove the team to the timber line along the river.

Awaiting them there were the McFalls, also dressed up. Buddy and Red, slicked up in Sunday suits, were wearing the felt hats Walking Owl brought them. Ruby's brown hair was arranged in braids on her head. She wore a new flowered dress with bonnet to match. And Dee Cee? Schell could hardly recognize her. Having never seen her in a dress, he stared in amazement at the young lady who smiled at him before she hopped gracefully into the back of the coverless wagon.

"Ain't she purty?" Buddy teased him.

"Now, Buddy, you cut that out. I'll git you if you don't act right." When everybody laughed, Dee Cee blushed.

Schell jumped down off the wagon to give his seat to Ruby. "Here Walker, you drive." He jerked his head at Martha to tell her to get in the back. "We *young* people will sit in the back."

At that the brothers laughed some more, teasing both Schell and Walking Owl.

"You boys mind yer manners, now." Ruby tried to be stern, but she too was affected by the holiday mood and giggled as Walking Owl beside her slapped the reins for the mules to move.

At the impromptu meeting grounds in the vacant lot next to the general store at Deerfield, people gathered from miles around. Neighbors who hadn't seen anyone for weeks greeted one another with hugs or hand shakes. Immediately the gathering split into three groups. The men smoked, whittled, and swapped news and tales. The women were even more actively sharing news, recipes, and admiring each others' new dresses made for the occasion. The children jabbed one another on the arms playfully, daring others to foot races or spontaneous jumping contests. It was a happy gathering of work-worn people, who had suffered years of privation and loss, coming together in fellowship and worship.

Schell and Walking Owl visited with the few men they knew from their infrequent trips to the village and met others from the outlying areas.

"Davis is the name," said one jovial newcomer. "Moved here from Cedar County about the time you come back.

You're Schell Campbell from Campbell's Hump, ain't you?"

"Right. This is my partner, Walker."

"Yeah, I've heard of you. Union soldiers, eh?" Davis said looking at the officer's hat Schell always wore and Walking Owl's army trousers and boots.

"Yeah, but that's over now."

"I hear they's outlaws out here don't think so."

"Haven't had any trouble in awhile now. Things are getting back to normal. Glad to have you as a neighbor."

When the preacher walked to the front, indicating time to start, in the shade of the few elms and black locusts people sat down on logs, blankets, or hickory-bottomed chairs they'd brought along. Walking Owl disappeared. Ruby, Martha, and the brothers joined some friends. Seeing an empty space on the log beside Dee Cee, Schell joined her. She smiled at him.

"You do look pretty," Schell whispered after several minutes of the long sermon.

Dee Cee grinned. Later while the congregation was singing, she said to Schell, "You've done a fine job here. I never thought Marthie would be so happy again."

Schell looked at her and smiled. A compliment from her? He started to wave it aside as nothing when she added, "No, I mean it. And what you've done fer Walker and all of us. We feel like we're part of the human race again, not jest hunted animals protectin' our dens."

For another hour the preacher's voice boomed over them, promising burning hell waters and eternal damnation if they didn't face up to their wickedness.

"Repent, sinners, come." Perspiration ran down the preacher's face and dripped off his chin. His shirt was wet through in his exertions during the two hours of his vociferous sermon. He paced up and down in front of the group. His eyes bulged at especially emotional points in his talk.

Then his voice became gentle, pleading as he invited people to join him in the front to repent. "Come up here and be washed clean with the blood of the lamb." Walking through the crowd, begging people one by one he cried, "Come, now before the fires of hell and damnation wash over you forever, casting you into an ever-burning pit."

When people started moaning and moving to the front, Schell motioned Dee Cee to slip out with him. They found a quiet, private spot to sit on the far side of the store building.

"Good thing the circuit rider doesn't come any oftener," Schell said. "I don't have the constitution to sit still that long."

Dee Cee giggled, "Me neither. But it's good to be with people again, laughin' and talkin'."

"Yeah, it sure is. I haven't been to church since in New York with Cynthia—all solemn, quiet, and proper-like in a huge vaulted church building." He waved his hands to encompass their outdoor meeting place where the preacher was circulating with exhortations and comfort through his moaning and shouting congregation. Overhead was the hot summer sky with not a single cloud to decorate their domed roof. Schell slapped at a persistent green-headed fly, and laughed. "But it sure wasn't like this."

"What would Cynthia think of this?"

Schell just threw out his hands. "Can you see her letting that preacher marry her?" He gave a short nervous laugh.

"Does it still hurt, her leavin' you like that?" Dee Cee asked seriously.

"Some. But not much anymore." He paused and looked at her. "Not anymore."

"Schell," Dee Cee said smiling, "did you realize that today for the first time each of us complimented the other?"

"That we did. Sort of a truce?"

"Yeah. You're all right. I reckon when you first come back that I sort of resented you, your ranch, your money, the infernal arrogance of your army lieutenant bearing."

Schell stared at her. "I resented you, too, your independence, your quickness . . ."

"Because I'm a woman?" Dee Cee interrupted. "You'd like me if I was the feller you first took me for." When Schell flinched, she added, "Wouldn't you?"

"Yes," Schell answered truthfully. "But I'm beginning to like you even better because you *are* a woman." He looked into her eyes in the bright light of midday. From the other side of the store, the voices of people at the meeting, singing and shouting their joy of finding God, orchestrated their conversation. "Can I give you that hug you wouldn't let me give you at Halley's Bluff?"

She nodded. The hug turned into a long kiss.

"Were you also mad with me because I was going to marry Cynthia?" Schell asked softly, running his hands over her hair.

Dee Cee stiffened. "No," she said quickly. "Well, yes, I guess so. I thought you were too smart to do a stupid thing like that."

Schell laughed. "I wasn't the smart one. Cynthia was.

She was the one who knew right off that it wouldn't work. Not me. Not then. I know now."

Schell looked at the lovely woman beside him. *Hang it*, he decided, *she has all the attributes I value in a woman.* Cynthia faded in comparison. "We should thank Cynthia."

"Why?"

"Because without her leaving, we wouldn't be here together, and I couldn't kiss you again." Dee Cee met him half way in another long kiss. "Isn't this rather sinful, us kissing here while souls are being saved over there," she half giggled.

"How can love be sinful. After all the killing, I bet God is smiling at us," Schell confirmed, kissing her quickly on the forehead and on her cheek. The long one he planned for her mouth was interrupted by Red and Buddy rounding the corner of the store building.

When they started to taunt their sister, Dee Cee said before they could say anything, "Mind yer own business. Now git out of here."

After the meeting was over, the women spread out on improvised boards and trestles the food they had brought for dinner. Walking Owl reappeared and ate with Ruby. Schell and Dee Cee filled their tin plates and sat down on an old quilt in the shade of the wagon.

Deciding that he should tell what he'd learned about the McFall land, Schell said, "Dee Cee, I looked through the court records the other day in Nevada City when waiting for you and the others to get there from Blue Mounds. Did you know that your father had no legal title to your land?"

Dee Cee jerked up, the chicken drumstick she was eating stopped half way to her mouth. "What! Are you sure?"

"Yes. Then later I had the lawyer to check it. There's nothing in the McFall name."

Dee Cee put her plate down. "Pa never filed?"

Schell shook his head. "Apparently not."

"Then we don't own. . . . All these years for nothin'?" She glanced quickly across the meeting area to Ruby who was happily chatting with Walking Owl. "And someone could come in and run us off? Legally?"

"Yes."

She jumped to her feet as if ready to fight the whole gathering. "And with a piece of paper take what them bushwhackers and soldiers with guns couldn't do in five years? What Pa and my brother and sister got killed for?"

Schell pulled her back down. "Take it easy. They aren't here," he said gently.

"Whose name is it listed under?" Her eyes sparked in anger. "Who has jumped claim on our land?"

"A speculator in the East. The lawyer is contacting him to see if it is for sale."

"Our land! Buy our own land!" The fight gone from her she said, "But what good would that do? We got no money." Her shoulders sagged. Her eyes were on the patch of black dirt in front of them worn bare by many feet. "Is there anything we can do?"

Schell put his arm around her. "Well, there's still some government land north and west of you. With the new Homestead law your mother could file on some of that now that she's head of the household."

"She wouldn't do it. It wouldn't be *her* land."

"You could do it for her or even in your own name."

Dee Cee shook her head as she looked again at her mother.

The gathering was breaking up, adjourning to the river for baptizing those converted that morning. Not wanting to be gone from the ranch any longer, Schell gathered up his group and pulled out early.

Walking Owl and Ruby sat close together on the driving seat. The brothers and Martha soon went to sleep. Schell held Dee Cee in his arms. For the first time in his life he wished home were farther away.

The road from Deerfield followed the section line straight south. It forded Big Dry Wood River a mile from the village and came out of the timber onto the prairie again. After moving at a walk for two more miles, Walking Owl increased the mules' pace to a trot. Schell held Dee Cee tightly to keep her from bouncing. Martha and the brothers grumbled to Walking Owl to slow down. But, instead of slowing, Walking Owl shook the reins, urging the team to go even faster.

Alarmed, Schell crawled the length of the wagon bed to the seat. "What's the matter?" Then he didn't need to hear the answer because he saw what had alarmed his partner. Over the horizon south of them, spiraled upward blue-gray smoke. Dee Cee grabbed Schell's arm. No one spoke, not even Martha or the boys, for they all feared the same thing. Schell, Dee Cee, and her brothers readied their guns. Ruby climbed into the back of the wagon to crouch behind the protection of the wooden wagon bed with Schell, Martha, and her family.

As they drew closer to the smoke, they knew their first fears were correct. The smoke came from the marshy land between the river and creek. Even as they approached, the smoke was dying down. Walking Owl slowed enough for Red and Buddy to drop off just before reaching the trail into the timber. A quarter of a mile farther, Schell and Dee Cee jumped off and disappeared into the trees. Walking Owl stopped the wagon just beyond the trail. He quickly unharnessed the team. Ruby and Martha climbed on one mule and he the other. Walking Owl lead off on a circuitous route around the denser portion of the marsh between the two streams. Though not easy riding, the mules were sure-footed and smart enough not to run blindly into entangling brush or fall into ditches.

Schell and Dee Cee reached the McFall clearing a few minutes before the others. What was once a house was now only smoldering ashes. They heard Red's all-clear whistle, immediately followed by Walking Owl's signal. Knowing there was no one there, the three groups converged on the clearing.

Still no one spoke. What was there to say? They each knew that bushwhackers had taken advantage of their absence to burn the house. Schell and Martha knew that their house had escaped this time because as they raced down the road, they had seen it still standing on The Hump. From the smoking remains of the fire Schell surmised that the bushwhackers had been gone for at least an hour. He put an arm around Martha and broke the silence. "They didn't get our house," he assured her.

Walking Owl had the same thoughts. "One of us ought to ride to The Hump to see about Si."

Schell nodded. "First let's see what we can do here."

Walking Owl stepped around the hot ashes of the fire looking carefully at the ground for tracks. Meanwhile Red returned from one set of outbuildings and Buddy from another to say that they had not been damaged, but the horses were gone.

Walking Owl picked up the trail of four riders and four riderless horses heading west.

"Let's go git 'em!" Red yelled, waving his arm for the others to follow as he ran.

"Red!" Ruby called. "Come back here. You know better'n to run off half-cocked like that."

Unwillingly he came back, "But Ma, they've got a good start of us."

"Yes," Walking Owl said softly, "but on foot you could never catch them."

Schell turned to Dee Cee. "I need to check at home, but if things are okay there, we are with you whatever you want to do."

"Git them scum that burned our house and stole our hosses," Red said. "That's what we want to do."

Dee Cee nodded. "And git back our ponies. This about knocks us out." She looked about ready to give up with this complete wipe-out on top of learning that they didn't own their land.

They agreed that while Dee Cee and the boys checked on their various caches, the others would take the mules and wagon back to The Hump and check on Si. The men would get horses, supplies, and gear for a possible overnight for the men and Dee Cee to track the bushwhackers. Ruby and Martha would keep the lookout on The Hump.

They found Campbell's Hump untouched. Very agitated, Si told them he had not seen any riders east of the river, further confirming that the bushwhackers went west. Knowing there was nothing he could do when he saw the smoke from the McFall house, Si had kept watch from The Hump.

Hearing the plans for tracking the outlaws included him,

Si stated, "I signed up to trap wolves. I ain't huntin' no outlaws. No sirree. Nor keepin' watch, neither. I quit."

Angry, Schell said, "Okay, get your gear and the skins you've trapped. Here's a half month's pay." Si grabbed the money and disappeared into the bunkhouse.

"We'll stay on their trail until we get them, Ruby," Schell said. From the moment she saw the smoke from her house, Ruby had held her mouth tight. Her eyes had lost the brightness of the earlier afternoon when she and Walking Owl sat close together on the wagon seat. The life had gone out of her face.

"We'll get your horses back," Walking Owl assured her.

"We're not going to sit home anymore hoping nobody will harm us. That's it! We'll get these vermin," Schell said. His heart ached, remembering all that Dee Cee and her mother had borne.

"Git goin'," Ruby said. "Go quickly before the trail gits any colder."

Martha handed Schell a pair of his old pants and shirt rolled up in a bundle. "For Dee Cee," she said. Schell remembered Dee Cee's clothing was burned up and she was dressed up in Sunday clothes. So was he. Quickly he changed into his working outfit.

"Be careful," Ruby called as the two men galloped over the ridge leading three other horses.

There was still a good four hours of light, when late in the July afternoon, they caught up with Dee Cee and her brothers. Finding their caches untouched, the McFalls had picked up the outlaws' trail where Walking Owl stopped tracking. They followed it on foot. The trail through the marsh was difficult to follow, but when it left the woods for the prairie, there was a wide swathe of the dried grass bent over and trampled from the many horses' hooves. The McFalls knew how to follow a trail, though not as skillful in tracking as Walking Owl, who could distinguish individual horse tracks.

The brothers and Dee Cee gladly mounted the horses Schell brought for them. With Walking Owl in the lead, they trotted across the prairie over land that he hoped to buy. However, his careful scrutiny of the land was not to assess its richness, but to read the tracks.

"They're moving at a slow lope," Walking Owl said. "I'd say about three hours ahead of us."

Schell glanced at the sun. "About that long until dark," he said.

"They'll probably hole up for the night before we can catch up to them," Walking Owl said.

"Better that way. They won't see us."

"Right." Walking Owl grinned. This time they might turn the tables and ambush genuine outlaws, not *be* ambushed.

"I can tell you I'm not anxious for a shoot-out on the prairie," Schell said.

Walking Owl agreed.

A mile farther down the trail, Dee Cee knelt beside him when he dismounted to study the tracks in a dusty, grassless spot. "Can you recognize our horses' tracks?" she asked.

"Yes. These tracks are from your ponies. They don't carry riders. Also, they all have the mark of the blacksmith at Deerfield—turned down heels on the back feet." He knelt down and pointed. "And this set of tracks here was made by Ruby's mare."

"How can you tell?"

"The mare does what they call a rope walk. Instead of her right and left feet tracks being apart and parallel to each other, they are almost in a line as if walking a tight rope. That's Ruby's mare. These are your horses, no question about that."

"And the other tracks?" Dcc Cee asked.

"These others are different. I know they carry riders, because they cut deeper into the ground. This horse's tracks are bigger." Walking Owl studied the track. "I'd say the horse is a good two hands taller than any of the others. Probably a stallion."

"Like that big sorrel the bushwhacker rode that chased down Schell's girl?"

Walking Owl raised his eyebrows at her question. "Yes, about that size. As big as that horse was. This horse is slightly pigeoned-toed. The farrier has tried to correct his toeing-in by adding weights."

For the first time since seeing her burned home, Dee Cee spoke with her accustomed spunk. "Then that *is* Hank Teller we're trailin'. He's ridin' Pa's sorrel he stole from us the night he killed . . ." Dee Cee did not finish.

"Red!" She mounted and caught up with her brother. "You were right. Last month when he was chasin' Schell's girl, Hank *was* ridin' Pa's sorrel like you said. Walker picked out his tracks."

Schell had to restrain the youth from galloping ahead after the outlaw.

Even though the group was traveling at a gentle lope, a larger group of horsemen was approaching them from behind. Since they were waving, one even held up a bandanna tied on the end of a stick, Schell and Walking Owl knew they were friendly. Though not stopping completely, Walking Owl slowed down for the group to catch them.

"Know them?" Schell asked Dee Cee.

Dee Cee studied the men. "Yeah. They are farmers from around Deerfield."

"That guy in front is Davis." Schell said when the group got close enough to recognize him. "I talked to him at the preaching."

"Campbell," Davis shouted. "Hold up."

The men told them that several other homes had been burned while everyone was at the meeting. Since the other families rode their horses to the preaching, only the McFalls lost their horses, but they each were robbed of something—cured meat, hides, money, whatever the bush-whackers could carry off. Everyone of them came home to a burned-out house, barn, or some building. The Davis place was first. He and his son tracked the bushwhackers to two more farms, gathering manpower at each stop, before they came to Campbell's Hump. They probably would have lost the tracks in the marshy bottom land if Ruby hadn't told them where to intercept Schell and Walking Owl.

"It's Hank Teller and his gang," Schell told them. "Walker figured it out from his horse's tracks."

The men's anger had increased as they rode. Learning that their prey was the local boy turned outlaw enraged them even more. Not only were they chasing an arsonist and a thief, but a killer, too.

"It's time we rid the county of varmin like him," Davis yelled.

"Since they ain't no law in the county, we got to do it ourselves," a large farmer agreed.

"A necktie party is too good fer him," one said whirling his lasso in the air.

"Yeah. What're we waitin' on? While's we're gabbin' they're gittin' away."

With that the newly formed vigilante group galloped on, Red and Buddy with them.

"Schell?" Dee Cee was impatient to join the others, but held back because the partners did. "You comin'?"

"They're very angry now and unorganized. Let them go, and good luck to them, but Walker and I work differently."

Walking Owl nodded. "Don't hold much for mobs." He tapped his finger on his forehead. "We use our heads."

The partners shaded their eyes against the sun as they watched the departing men, almost hidden by the dust they stirred up. Walking Owl scanned the whole western horizon. "That Teller fellow is headed straight to Kansas," he said. "Dee Cee, you know this country. Where do you reckon he's headed? He sure seems sure of himself."

"Hank ain't very smart. He probably thinks we won't cross the state line since we never did before, and he's got enough lead to reach it before we catch him." She thought for a few seconds. "I agree with you, Walker, that he'll go straight to Kansas. Now ever'thing west is open prairie, and north is Ft. Scott. He'll sure not go that direction. Across the border he'll probably turn south to where there's some rough land. I ain't been there in a couple of years, but Pa used to take us trappin' there some."

"Good," Schell said, "if we cut across southwesterly now, we might find the trail ahead of that bunch up there." He pointed to the ten men just disappearing over the rise.

"But Red and Buddy?" Dee Cee asked.

"They'll be all right," Schell assured her. "Remember

they are almost men now. They know how to take care of themselves."

"And if we don't find Hank Teller, the boys will catch up with him, anyway." Dee Cee agreed that it was a good idea to work in two separate groups.

"Exactly," Schell said. "Lead the way, Dee Cee. You know this country."

The three turned southwesterly into the hot wind that blew almost constantly across the unending grasses during the hot summer days.

## Chapter Eleven

There was just enough light left for Walking Owl to see the ground as he, Schell, and Dee Cee rode their horses at an easy walk on the level grassland across the Kansas border. After heading southwest for a few miles, Dee Cee had turned straight west, hoping to cut across Hank Teller's trail just north of the hilly, tree-covered area. They were hurrying along the fringes of the rough land, trying to intercept the trail before it became too dark to see.

"It oughta be around here somewhere," Dee Cee said in exasperation after many minutes of searching. Perhaps their hunch was wrong, and they should have continued following the trail with the farmers. If they didn't find Hank Teller tonight, they had very little hope of catching him or finding their horses. Darkness now might prevent them from locating the gang, though it would give them protection if they did.

The three were spread out over the rolling ground, leaning down from the saddles studying the surface beneath them. When they came to the road which Dee Cee said marked the westernmost boundary of the route the gang would have taken if they were headed to the hills, Schell was ready to back-track; they must have missed the trail. He had already started back when Walking Owl whistled to get his attention and then gestured him to come.

The Osage was kneeling in the dust of the hard dirt road surface. Although there were tracks of many horses coming and going, he picked out the pigeon-toed stallion's track. Hank Teller had boldly ridden down this well-used road. Obviously he did not fear pursuit. Walking Owl stepped down the road a few rods studying the tracks.

"Just walking now," he said. "About an hour ahead of us."

"What route would he take from the road to get to the hilly area?" Schell asked Dee Cee.

She tried to remember the trails. "About a mile down here there's a path that leads back into the woods to a dry creek and slough."

"Would that be a good place to pass the night?" Schell asked.

Dee Cee nodded.

The last reflected light in the red-orange clouds scattered in the west was slowly waning. Hoping to find the outlaws before the light was completely gone, the three loped down the road. Walking Owl watched for tracks going off the right side of the road and Schell the left just in case the outlaws had veered off. Dee Cee swept the southern horizon for any dust, campfire smoke, or other evidence.

When they reached the trail into the hilly area, it was too dark to see tracks. Without light, and not wanting to give away their presence by building a fire, they rested their mounts in a sumac draw near the road and waited for the moon to rise. Since the total area around the dry creek was less than 200 acres, they figured that they could hear the bushwhackers or see their firelight if they were camped there.

After watering the horses in a seep in the draw, Schell pulled out some dried meat and bread from his saddlebags. Cicadas overhead never ceased their sing-song, monotonous noise. A lone meadowlark called. When the wind died down in the evening, the mosquitoes appeared in droves. Slapping away the troublesome insects, they watched the almost-full moon clear the trees in the east.

"Now," Schell said. With their horses tethered, they each went separate ways to comb the area. The plan was that in one half hour they were to return to this spot to reconnoiter if necessary.

It wasn't necessary. Schell found the camp first. The bushwhackers were so keyed up with their success that they were laughing and chatting loudly enough that Dee Cee and Walking Owl soon heard them from their positions farther away. By giving their bird call signals, the friends were soon together again on a small hill overlooking the dry slough where the outlaws were camped. About fifty feet from the campfire, all of the horses, including the McFalls', were tied to a picket rope strung between two pin oaks.

The bushwhackers' raucous voices carried through the night, though the three watchers could not distinguish the words. They watched for several minutes, studying the layout of the land, noticing where the men laid their guns, and where they piled their loot. The friends were looking for the best paths in and out, and thinking what to do. By now the moon was shining through the tree branches, making splattered blotches of light and darkness. In their tawny and brown clothes the three blended into the background.

Schell and Walking Owl were thinking alike—steal back the horses as they did at Blue Mounds. But the problem this time was more than simply mounting their horses and getting away without being seen. This time there were eight horses to sneak out right from under the noses of the gang. In addition to getting the horses, they needed to return and capture the outlaws.

"Each one of us get one horse at a time?" Schell asked his partner.

"It'd take three trips," Walking Owl whispered back.

Though they didn't tell Dee Cee what they meant, she understood. She said softly, "They are drinking now. Wait until they get drunk and go to sleep."

Agreed that waiting was the best plan, Schell and Dee Cee tried to relax while Walking Owl kept the first watch. At least the mosquitoes were not as bad on the hill. Dee Cee drew close to Schell and leaned against him as he put his arm around her. They kissed. This was not the place to talk; they had no need for words.

When the moon was almost straight overhead, giving them the brightest light of the night, Dee Cee and Schell crept silently after Walking Owl. Close enough to hear the heavy, regular breathing of the sleeping bushwhackers, they circled around the low area to approach the horses from the far side of the slough. Without discerning which horse it was, they each untied the lead rope of the nearest horse. Dee Cee pointed to the pile of loot taken from the settlers. Schell shook his head. Later, he indicated. The task now was to secure the McFall horses and remove the outlaws' mounts so they could not easily escape or come after them.

Stroking the horses to calm them, they each held their hands over their horse's nose to keep it from snorting, and led it very slowly and carefully out of earshot. Then more quickly, they returned to the draw where their own horses were tied.

They made the second trip without incident. While the partners returned for the final two horses, Dee Cee rigged up ropes to help lead out the extra horses. Two of them would have a string of three horses—a bit of a problem for saddle horses not used to being led in that manner. This part of the escape would probably be the most difficult. She searched through their saddle bags for anything to cover the horses' heads to make them easier to handle.

The partners returned with the last two horses. "Maybe we should not try to take them away all at once," Schell suggested. They had a total of eleven horses to move. Thinking that each of them could lead out two horses apiece, they decided to take out first the four McFall horses and the big sorrel. They would leave the remaining three bushwhacker horses securely tied to the trees.

Dee Cee strapped her saddle on her father's stallion, climbed on, and leading her rescued pinto and the horse she had borrowed from Schell, she led the way out onto the road.

"Now let's get some help," Schell said. The others readily agreed. They backtracked down the road about a mile until they found the farmers' camp.

The eight farmers-turned-vigilantes and the McFall brothers had followed the outlaws' trail to the road. With easy traveling from there, they made good time. However, darkness overtook them before they reached the hideout. Unable to track in the dark, they had stopped for the night, not realizing how close they were to the outlaws' camp.

Immediately the men were awake and raring to go. Schell and Davis could barely restrain them. Only Walking Owl's menacing six foot, eight figure and booming voice quieted them so that they could listen after Schell filled them in on what the three had done.

"Shut up! Listen to our plan," Schell said. "First we want to get out the rest of their horses. Without horses they can't go far."

"They are drunk asleep now, without any idea anyone is after them," Walking Owl said.

Davis suggested, "They'll stay there the night, so why not get someone to ride to Ft. Scott for the Bourbon County sheriff. Let him catch them."

That suggestion was shouted down quickly.

"He won't come. We're not even from the same state."

"Hank Teller ain't broke the law here."

"The sheriff couldn't git here quick enough."

"It's our homes that are burned. Let's git him."

"He killed my Pa and my brother and sister," Red yelled.

"Okay," Schell agreed, silencing the men again. "Okay. We'll capture them ourselves. Now, here's the plan. Let Dee Cee and Buddy McFall go after the rest of the horses. When they are clear, then we will surround their camp."

When everyone agreed to that plan, Dee Cee and Buddy raced ahead to get the horses before any noise the men made might alert the bushwhackers. Schell, Walking Owl, and the rest of the farmers followed more slowly. Just before turning off the road onto the trail, Schell once again went over the plan. Part 1: Spread out on the hills above the camp to surround it. Part 2: Remove the outlaws' guns. Part 3: Capture the outlaws.

His last whispered command to the eight men huddled around him was, "Remember. Do not shoot. Walker, Red, and I will disarm them. There will be no need for any killing. We have enough manpower here to capture them alive with no one getting hurt."

When he heard some grumbling from a man in the back, Schell repeated. "Davis, you are in charge. Men, again, wait for the order before going in. I'll give the bobwhite call. Then, Davis, give the order to go in after them. The rest should be easy."

"Right," Davis said glad to give the leadership responsibility to this experienced army man. As the partners and Red slipped into the woods, Davis ordered the men where to station themselves to wait for Schell's signal.

Walking Owl and Red followed Schell to the slough where the outlaws were sleeping. Schell crawled into the camp area to three rifles that were stacked against a tree just a few feet from one of the bushwhackers. Lying on his stomach four feet behind him was Walking Owl. Red was four feet behind the Osage. One at a time Schell passed the rifles to Walking Owl, who passed them to Red. When Red had all three, he retreated up the hill. His job done, he lay on his stomach, uncocked his own shotgun, and held Hank Teller in his sights.

Schell retrieved the fourth rifle, which was lying on the ground beside one of the men, and stuffed into his own belt two pistols he pulled from holsters hanging from tree limbs.

Walking Owl meanwhile had the more difficult task of

getting the two remaining pistols from holsters still strapped around the sleeping outlaws' waists. He inched over to the warm ashes of the fire beside Hank Teller, who was lying on his back. His pistol was snapped in its holster which was fastened to his belt and tied to his leg. The moonlight glinted on the silver handle as Hank moaned in his sleep and turned on his side. His leg covered his gun. Walking Owl waited patiently.

Apparently the position was uncomfortable, for Hank groaned again and flopped back. Walking Owl's hand darted out. The next time Hank turned over to his side he remained in that position for there was no pistol in his holster.

There was one final pistol to get. Walking Owl slithered on his stomach to the outlaw farthest from the campfire site. Just as Walking Owl was reaching to pull the pistol out of its holster, one of the farmers on the hill above him slipped. A cascade of rocks tumbled down the little ravine, clattering and falling into the midst of the bushwhackers.

The outlaws jumped up shouting and swearing at the ambush and finding their guns missing. A volley of shots came from the hills above them. The outlaw who still had a pistol shot blindly into the trees. There was much crashing in the underbrush. Schell yelled, "Cease fire!" Davis hollered himself hoarse, "Hold your fire. Don't shoot." All the men, outlaws and vigilantes, cried out, whooped, and cursed.

Not until the guns were empty was it quiet enough to hear Schell's stentorian military order. "Cease fire!"

A quick glance showed him that the place where he last saw Walking Owl was vacant. He let out a sigh. His partner got out before being struck by the rain of bullets. His next glance was the spot on the hillside where Red still lay, his gun in his hands unfired. As he scanned the scene, he saw Dee Cee and Bud crouched on the crest of the hill, guns ready, but like Red's unfired.

Then he assessed the damage as the farmers gathered in the bushwhackers' camp. Three outlaws were dead, their bodies sprawled on the ground, their faces frozen in masks of surprise and horror. Hank Teller was still alive, though bleeding from an arm wound. One of the vigilantes was injured, not from the outlaw's shots, but from falling down the ravine. He carefully got to his feet and limped into the campsite.

Schell raised to his full six feet height, his eyes flashing anger, his thick black hair streaming. The moonlight highlighted his white face framed with his beard. There was sudden silence as he looked from man to man in the group around him. His presence commanded attention. "I told you not to fire until I gave the word." He spoke each word slowly and distinctly as an officer chastising his men.

He turned to Davis, "See to this man's wounds," he pointed his foot at Hank Teller, "and tie him up. We'll take him to Ft. Scott where there is still some law."

At that the men rebelled.

"They'll jest turn him loose."

"We ain't in the army. Since when can you give orders?"

"We can't let vermin like this live."

"Let's hang him!"

Whatever control Schell had over them evaporated. He looked at Davis, who threw up his hands in defeat.

"Davis," Schell said, "we'll leave the outlaws' horses

back at your camp—all except the sorrel they stole from the McFalls a couple of years ago. Do what you can here."

Davis nodded. "Thanks, Campbell. By ourselves we'd never have caught up with them."

Followed by Red, Schell climbed up the hill to Dee Cee and Bud. Walking Owl was already there.

"Let's get the horses and go home," Schell said sadly. "I can't take any more killing." He waved his hand back toward the slough where the men were manhandling the wounded outlaw. Removing his hat and wiping his forehead with his bandanna, the anger in his voice barely in control, Schell added, "I want no part in that."

Red was shaking, tears running down his face, wanting to leave, but unable to take his eyes off the scene in the slough. Dee Cee put her arms around him. "Dee Cee, it was like that night when Hank Teller shot Pa and Bob and Nellie."

"I know, Red. Yes, I know."

"It was like they was gittin' killed all over again. Shot at from the timber at night with no warnin'."

Tears were rolling down Dee Cee's cheeks also. "Yes, Red, jest like it. Like hunted animals."

"I thought I could kill Hank Teller. I've hated him all this time, jest waitin' 'til I could kill him." Red wiped the tears from his eyes with the back of his dirty shirt sleeve. "But I couldn't. I had him in my sights, but I couldn't pull the trigger."

"I had him in my sights, too," Dee Cee said. "Neither could I."

"But a woman's not supposed to. I'm a man, and I couldn't."

Walking Owl put his hand lightly on Red's shoulder.

"Knowing when to kill and when to hold your fire is the measure of a man. Shooting an unarmed man from ambush, even one as evil as Hank Teller, is not manly. Your going into their camp and removing the rifles right under their noses was man's work. You can count on that."

"I'd have killed him if he'd a-got you," Red said.

"I know. I felt safe knowing you covered me," Walking Owl said, patting Red's shoulder.

Down in the slough two men were putting a noose around Hank Teller's neck. Another was up in a tree, looping the other end of the rope over a branch. Hank Teller was crying out, begging, offering the men gold, anything they wanted, not to hang him.

"Let's get out of here," Schell said, his face a mask to hold in his own emotions. His arm around Dee Cee, he turned his back to the scene. Walking Owl pulled the mesmerized brothers away.

They hurried to their mounts, and leading the recovered horses, they cut across the moonlit prairie in a beeline for Campbell's Hump.

## Chapter Twelve

A week later Schell, Walking Owl, Ruby, Dee Cee, and Martha were eating the noon meal Ruby had spread out on a quilt on the courthouse lawn. The dog, Harris, lay quietly watching his charges and hoping for some scraps. Schell's wagon was parked on Walnut, the "street" on the north side of the square. Once again Nevada City was looking like a town. Two new stores had been built on the square. There was a barber shop, the newspaper office, a bank, a lumber yard, a livery, a blacksmith, a saloon. Even a doctor had set up his office above one of the stores. The four unpaved streets forming the square each had some businesses. People were moving back. Almost daily some-one started a new house. The newspaper editor estimated that by 1870 there would be eleven thousand people in the county.

The showers the past few days had settled the dust in the streets. There were ruts cut by the wagon wheels and muddy spots pedestrians had to bypass to avoid sinking into the mud. In contrast to the usual hot, dry wind, a breeze from the scattering clouds brushed Schell's face and stirred Ruby's sunbonnet strings.

There was much talk in the town about the bushwhackers, not only about Hank Teller's gang, but others over the county. There had been several murders, with the criminals still roaming the county or escaping to Kansas when pursuers got close.

"We've got to get some law and order," said a businessman whose store had been robbed two times.

Groups of men and women gathered on the weedy lawn in the middle of the square where the courthouse once stood. Others talked in the barber shop or the saloon.

The little group from Campbell's Hump were not as interested in the buzz around them as they were in talking over the results of their trip to town and the exciting futures of all of them.

First, the legal work on Schell and Martha's inheritance was completed. The four parcels of land, including Campbell's Hump, was transferred to them. Brother and sister signed the documents, receiving the deed. After admiring it, Schell put it into a fireproof vault in the new bank for safekeeping.

Next, Walking Owl completed the paperwork for filing on his 160-acre homestead. The land investment company that owned the rest of the land he wanted, after hearing about all the raids and burnings in the county, was glad to sell at $1.50 an acre. They authorized the lawyer to sell what he could. Walking Owl bought the 480 acres next to his homestead claim, giving him a section of land adjoining the Campbell's west boundary and north of the McFalls. It was exactly what he wanted, virgin prairie bisected by the snaky, wooded line of Big Dry Wood River.

Their next problem was the McFall land.

When the men and Dee Cee returned from Kansas with the horses, Ruby, though freed at long last from the menace of Hank Teller, was despondent on learning that she did not own her land. Even after the murders of her husband and two children, she had held on the last two years, sustained by her determination to give her remaining sons and Dee Cee the start in life she and Mac envisioned for them. That start meant land—the means of supporting themselves and a home no one could force them to leave.

The house burning was a setback, but having anticipated that might happen, Ruby was prepared. Even though the family lost their house and its furnishings, some clothing and other valuables had been stashed in their various hideouts. She could handle losing the house; it was replaceable. She could not cope with losing the land.

During the last week, everyone at The Hump had pitched in to help the McFalls put together a makeshift house. Ruby went through the motions, cooking and otherwise tending to daily work, though her zest was gone. Her mood affected everyone. Neither the return of Mac's sorrel, nor Walking Owl's good fortune with his furs could erase the gloom of the people on Big Dry Wood.

Dee Cee took the leadership. She knew that they must face the land problem squarely. With Schell's and Walking Owl's help, she persuaded her mother to go to town to see what could be done.

The lawyer confirmed that Mac had not filed. Yes, a speculator back east did claim the land.

Ruby shrugged and said to her daughter, "What's the use?" Then to the lawyer, "When do we have to git off?"

The lawyer was thinking what to reply when Schell asked, "When did that fellow file on their land?"

"August, 12, 1864."

"How could that be?" Dee Cee asked angrily, standing up. "There was no land office here then. No government representatives or officials. And the official records weren't even in the county then. The courthouse was burned the year before that, but the court records were saved and eventually stored in Ft. Scott 'til after the war."

The lawyer looked at Dee Cee with respect. "You're right! This claim can't be legal."

Sitting up a bit straighter, Ruby looked from one to the other, not daring to hope. "What does that mean?"

The group waited impatiently as the lawyer read through the papers scattered on his desk and referred several times to books on his shelf. "It means," he said after a few minutes, "that this fellow has no legal claim to the land. He forged the papers."

"Then it's ours?" Ruby asked. Her sparkle returned.

"Not exactly. I believe that I can prove that it is still public land. Then you and your son, here," he looked at Dee Cee, "You're over twenty-one, aren't you?"

"Yes. I'm twenty-three," Dee Cee said.

The lawyer continued, "You, Mrs. McFall, and your son can each file for one hundred sixty acres under the Homestead Act."

Ruby's face lit up. "I've got a boy at home that'll be twenty-one in September."

The lawyer was as excited as the group before him. "Good. Get him in here. I'll file for the three of you. The fact that you have been living on the land continuously since 1841 will help prove your case."

The group was smiling as the lawyer pulled out papers and instructed them what to do. "One added thing," he said. "What were you during the war?"

"What do you mean?" Ruby asked.

"Were you Union or Rebel? Did any of your family fight on either side?"

"No. The boys were too young."

"Which side were you on?"

When Ruby looked puzzled, Dee Cee said. "We've been proud of the United States ever since my great-grandpa come over from Scotland. We've always been fer the Union, but all durin' the war in this county, we had to hide or be killed."

"Good," the lawyer said, busily writing everything down. "Now, Mrs. McFall, with you and your two sons, your family can claim four hundred and eighty acres. There will be a filing fee of ten dollars each. In five years, if you prove residence, you will get the title."

"We'll git the money," Dee Cee said.

"We've got enough furs fer that," Ruby agreed.

"Then, I'll go ahead and file for three of you."

Walking Owl said, "And I'll buy the remaining quarter of that section." He rose, his head almost touching the ceiling of the low room, walked to the wall map, and tapped his finger on the acreage he meant. "This piece that borders mine." When the others were puzzled, he added, "It'll be a wedding present."

Schell's mouth flew open. Ruby blushed and looked down at her hands neatly folded in her lap.

"Whose wedding?" Schell stammered.

Walking Owl looked at Ruby who nodded.

"Mine, I reckon," Ruby said looking at her daughter. "Walker and I have talked about marrying."

"And with both of us now landowners, there's nothing to stop us," Walking Owl said proudly.

Ruby smiled, nodded her agreement, and repeated, "Nothing."

Martha flew to Ruby and hugged her. Dee Cee put her hand over her mother's and squeezed it. Seeing the tears in her mother's eyes, Dee Cee reached into the back pocket of her trousers for a red bandanna handkerchief.

Schell was grinning broadly and pumping his partner's hand.

"Looks like you have their permission," the lawyer said to Walking Owl.

Schell returned to his seat by Dee Cee and took her hand. Pushing back her hat, he ran his hand lightly over her tousled boyish-cut hair, and looked into her bright eyes. Everyone in the room was watching him when he asked Dee Cee tenderly, "Shall we make it a double wedding?"

"What!" The lawyer jumped up, banging his knee on the desk and upsetting some papers.

The room reverberated with laughter. Walking Owl slapped his thighs in his merriment. Ruby's eyes danced with glee. Martha clapped her hands. Dee Cee was too amused to blush.

"Dee Cee is a *woman*, Mr. Carter," Schell said, suppressing his laughter, "not a man."

Mr. Carter fell back into his chair mumbling in embarrassment. "I'm . . . Sorry . . . The trousers . . . The name . . ."

"Don't fret, Mr. Carter," Dee Cee said. "I *am* a woman. Everybody makes the same mistake."

"Including me when I first got back home," Schell laughed.

To take the attention off of himself, and joining in on the general good feelings in the room, the lawyer turned to Dee Cee, "Well, young *woman*, you haven't answered the gentleman's question."

"I'll have to think about that." She paused, grinning at everyone, before turning to Schell. "Okay, I've thought about it. A double weddin' would be nice."

It was understandable why the happy and excited group were enjoying their meal in the shade of a scraggly cottonwood tree by Schell's wagon. They were too wrapped up in their own good fortune over the land deals and the happy future plans to pay much attention to the agitated townspeople around the town square.

"We will now all be one family, won't we, Schell?" Martha said. She was stroking Harris, who leaned against her leg.

"And Dee Cee and Red and Buddy will truly be my sister and brothers?" she asked Ruby.

"Yes, dearie." Ruby said.

"And Walker," Schell said, mischief in his eyes, "Will be my father-in-law."

Walking Owl grunted playfully.

"What will that make him to me?" Martha asked.

"Your friend, Martha, always your friend," Walking Owl said.

Relaxing after their meal and enjoying the freshness of the air after the rain, they began to be aware of the animated conversations around them. They heard words such as, "law and order," "murder," "growing town of Nevada City," "vigilantes," "hangings," and "sheriff."

Davis of Deerfield marched toward Schell from the largest gathering of townspeople and farmers where someone was giving a speech. Ignoring Harris's growls, and without greeting or other introduction, Davis demanded, "You ain't one of them radical Republicans, are you?"

Surprised at the question, Schell didn't answer right away. Davis continued, "I figured you'd support the Conservative Party here in the county. It's made up of the Democrats who can vote, and conservative Republicans."

Schell knew that the new State Constitution *forbad* anyone who participated in any way in the Southern cause from holding office or voting. But he couldn't figure out what Davis was getting at.

"Primaries are next month," Davis continued. "First election in the county in five years. We're gonna to have some law and order around here. And we need a sheriff."

"I agree," Schell said still mystified.

"Then we want you to run on our ticket," Davis said. Several men had gathered around Schell. "We was impressed with how you caught that Hank Teller gang. We think you'd beat that Williams feller from over east."

"I don't have any interest in running for office."

"It's yer patriotic duty. The county needs you," one of the men said.

"I've done my part. Let that Williams, whoever he is, do it if he wants the job. I don't." Schell's voice was firm.

Davis was disappointed. The men around him grumbled. "Then that feller over there," Davis pointed to a stout man talking to a gathering crowd on the corner of Walnut and Main. "That Williams will sure git it. Little good that'll do us in the west part of the county."

A familiar sounding voice penetrated Schell's awareness. Looking up, he nudged Walking Owl, who grinned back. He, too recognized the speaker. The partners and the women sauntered over to the group.

"Vote fer me fer sheriff, folks. I'll rid the whole county of outlaws jest as I did in my township. Me and my neighbors patrolled our neighborhood, keeping everyone safe fer *four*," he held up four fingers to emphasize the enormity of the deed, "fer four days and nights when the notorious bandits, *Frank and Jesse James* were holed up in a cave on the Osage River."

Walking Owl poked Schell in the ribs and said in an undertone to the women, "Dick, the-savior-of-his-community-against-non-existent-outlaws."

Schell snickered. The women could hardly contain their laughter. Martha had to hold her hand over her mouth.

The would-be sheriff noticed the women's smiles and pointed to them. "Now there's nothin' funny about being murdered in yer beds at night and havin' outlaws steal hosses out of yer barn while you're in bed sleepin'. If I am elected Sheriff, the whole county can sleep again without fear."

"Let's get out of here," Schell said.

Dee Cee touched his arm to hold him. She couldn't resist asking, "And how do you know that the James Brothers were ever there?"

"Because, young man, I seen them with these two eyes o' mine, a-ridin' down the road by my house *in broad daylight*."

"But how do you know they stayed four days," she taunted him.

"We seen their tracks. We found their hideout, *and*," he paused for the pièce de résistance, "we discovered what they were doing there all that time."

"What?" a youth in the audience asked.

Dick Williams made himself as tall as his short stature would allow, threw back his shoulders and said proudly, "They came to Halley's Bluff to dig up the gold they had buried there." There was a general murmur though the crowd.

"On the fourth day after spottin' 'em, we found pits in the bluff they had covered over sloppy-like. See," Dick leaned over to the crowd as if letting them in on a secret, "some time before, they had stashed their gold in them pits the fur traders used to use. The people living there on the bluff moved in recently and didn't know nothin' about them pits. The James Gang had covered their gold over with rotten furs and put dirt over all!"

The crowd expressed its admiration for such cleverness. Dick continued, his election in the bag, "And *I*, folks, I found the pits where the notorious criminals that have killed men in banks and trains, dug up their blood money and run. I seem them pits with my own eyes."

Schell's group returned quickly to the wagon to leave town so they could let out their laughter. As they passed by Dick Williams still speaking to his audience, Schell pulled Solomon up beside the candidate, touched the brim of his hat and said, "Schell Campbell from Campbell's Hump. We need a good sheriff. You've got my vote. Good luck."

Dick glanced briefly at Schell. "Thank you," he said and returned to his speech making.

Followed by Harris, Schell and Dee Cee rode their horses beside his wagon which was loaded with building and ranching supplies. By squinting his eyes into the southwest sun, he could make out Campbell's Hump, glimmering in the sunshine breaking through the clouds. Though he was too far away to see it, he *knew* that his modest house was on the mound and watched over by the McFall brothers, and his cattle were fattening on the range.

With him were the people he most cared about—Walking Owl, Ruby, and Martha were crowded together on the high wagon seat. "Frank," he teased Walking Owl, "what are you going to do with all your gold?"

Walking Owl's black eyes danced. Holding the reins in his right hand, he put his free arm around Ruby. "Retire from a life of crime, Jesse, and settle down."

Schell glanced over to Dee Cee riding her pinto close beside him. He reached out his free hand to take hers, squeezed it, and said, still looking at her, "Sounds like a fine idea."

They unconsciously quickened their pace. Scattered in the mature grasses were white blossoms of yarrow. Red gay feather spikes danced in the breeze, and in spots the black-eyed susans formed a yellow mass. Towering over even the tallest of the bluestem and switchgrass were the sunflowers, their yellow heads turned southwesterly.

So tranquil. After years of danger, the calm of the prairie enfolded Schell. Perhaps now there was peace in their borderland home; perhaps Walking Owl could live in harmony with his Great Mystery Force.

"Yahoo," Schell yelled, waving his hat in the air. He spurred Solomon to a canter. Beside him, her pinto matching each hoof beat, glided Dee Cee, her hat hanging by its strings down her back, her hair bouncing on her forehead. From directly behind them came Walking Owl's Osage yell of triumph, Harris's excited barking, and happy laughter from Ruby and Martha.